I0451356

Pieces of the Whole

By

AJ BLANC

White-Knight Press

Copyright © 2017 by Andrew White

Library of Congress Control Number: 2017915276

Print ISBN   978-0-9994574-0-5
Ebook ISBN   978-0-9994574-1-2

Written and published in the United States of America

Acknowledgements

This was a project three years in the making, almost to the day. It started as a way to pass the time, but soon become something I felt had a value that is worthwhile to share and turn into a series.

I have a great deal of gratitude for my editors, professional or otherwise: Christel Hall, my wife Monica, and my brother Robbie. There were others, who I am also thankful for, but those above gave me more tangible feedback and I can't thank them enough. I'm also quite pleased with the cover by Dafeenah Jameel at indiedesignz.com.

There are quite a few references and easter eggs to multiple works of science fiction, due to the many sources of inspiration I had for this book. From a fan of the genre to those who notice at least some of these homages, I salute you.

DRAMATIS PERSONAE

Harold "Hal" Dune, Medical Doctor &
      Licensed Forensic Technician

Kimber Lee, Inspector - Missing & Unidentified
      Persons Division

Miles Shepard, Bio-tech CEO

Jon Colquitt, SFPD Detective

Erwin Mutara, Forensic Pathologist

Martin Tucker, USCG Analyst

Aramis Navoa, Former VA employee

Monica Schell, Veterans Administration
      Hiring Manager

Sidney Leyton, Bio-tech CFO

Kestra Katarn, Bio-tech Administrator

Felinda Willrow, Patient Services Specialist

Tiberius Secura, Departmental Manager

Drinian Posey, Diagnostic Technician

Sabien El Fadil, Bio-tech Security Chief

Keyan Dannik, Military Contractor

Slade Wilkins, Lieutenant Regional Governor

Colonel William Kithe, USAF Commanding Officer

PROLOGUE: DEATH OF A STRANGER
2074 REALIGNMENT PERIMETER

His lungs burned, but he didn't stop running. The glare from the blanket of snow was blinding, but as long as he didn't turn around or stumble, the exact direction he ran was unimportant at this point. He knew he should be crossing the border at any moment. His heart pounded so loudly he feared he may not hear the perimeter drones; the sound of their stun bolts would be unmistakable though. Normally, people try to avoid being intercepted by overprotective drones. This time it might just be his salvation.

The sprinting, stately figure in a fox red Vicuña wool, turtleneck and charcoal slacks and shoes gave in to anxiety and glanced back to see if the company's internal security guardsmen were still pursuing him. Their dark-grey electronic dampening stealth suits were in stark contrast to the dazzling white that stretched in every direction. The guardsmen appeared to be falling behind, which would be a hopeful thought if he weren't still in the Realignment Region.

Momentary despair allowed fatigue to finally take over, waned. The movement of his legs turned erratic as his vision blurred. He noticed a black spot on the horizon gradually getting larger. The sight caused his stride to slow further as he considered that all the exertion was potentially making him delirious.

He stopped to briefly catch his breath and shake off the momentary lapse in coherence. After a few deep breaths, he looked up and relief flooded over him like a tidal wave when he realized what he was seeing wasn't a hallucination.

One perimeter drone stopped about ten meters in front of him. Its reverse tear-drop shape looked menacing despite its diameter being no larger than a soccer ball. A second drone circled around the area in a wide arc, as if it were a scavenger laying claim to its territory.

Instinctively the man sluggishly put his hands up to surrender, but his arms froze in place half-way up, paralyzed by the drone's stun bolt. He toppled over on his right side, like a mannequin being unintentionally bumped at a shopping center. Miraculously, he somehow managed to display a triumphant smile before he lost consciousness.

The two pursuers also stopped, as if they were struck by a stun bolt as well, but their deceleration was for another reason entirely. The guardsmen assumed their EDS suits would prevent detection by most drone scanners, but they had no desire to test the suit's limits by making unnecessary movements.

As the pair's quarry tumbled to the ground, and the drones awaited the collection detail to retrieve him, they considered their options. Their orders were to bring the deceitful doctor back to the labs, preferably alive. As long as the data he carried was retrieved, his condition was of no consequence. Now that he was in the custody of the Agrarians, with drones hovering over him, the likelihood of sensitive corporate information being released remained a significant risk. They knew they had to take action.

Almost robotically, they slowly turned their heads to face each other. The more senior of the two gave the other a subtle nod, with the reply being a noticeable sigh, though because of the suits' rebreathers no visible breath escaped.

Like a predator methodically stalking its prey, the subordinate guardsman slowly reached for his sidearm. He selected his preferred ordinance setting of bio-fletch, aimed, and fired its toxic projectile into his grinning target.

ONE: BUSINESS AS USUAL
SAN FRANCISCO, GOOGLE REGION

It was raining again. Not the typical Bay Area drizzle; a genuine downpour. We sure could've used this fifty years ago when the state barely got any rain for over a decade, and the already distressed agricultural communities nearly collapsed, Hal thought to himself. Luckily, between a surge of synthesized foods and more industrial water purifiers, California was able to repeal the Population Control Act of 2037 in less than twenty years after it was imposed.

His eyes darted suspiciously from his small coffee to the street vendor who eyed him contemptuously. He wondered how much longer he could pretend to prepare his now lukewarm beverage under the corner café's canopy before getting asked to leave.

He considered telling the weathered Asian woman that he was waiting to hear from a potential employer and didn't want to receive the news soaking wet on the street. However, judging by the lack of customer seating and expeditiousness of the other patrons, he figured she wouldn't find that an acceptable reason for lingering as long as he had.

To avoid an inevitable tongue-lashing if he remained a moment more, he snapped a lid on his well-stirred drink, held his flex-tablet over his head in an overly dramatic manner, so the barista would notice, and stepped out into the deluge. The ultra-thin, predominantly translucent tablet made for a surprisingly adequate umbrella. As Hal navigated the congested sidewalk, he wondered if the tablet's designers considered an umbrella as an ulterior function.

Although Hal had visited San Francisco many times, for various reasons, he had only lived there for four weeks and still didn't know the city well. Though he didn't recall the source, he remembered reading that some long-time residents of San Francisco were able to accurately pinpoint where they were in the city based on smell alone. Thanks to the rain, the putrid odor of soiled food and dank trash imprinted that aroma firmly in his mind as he scurried through the area.

He was barely a block from the street café when his wrist mobile vibrated to let him know he had a new message. Hal glanced up and down the street, hoping to find at least a somewhat dry place to retrieve the message, but all he saw were over-crowded awnings and unwelcoming entrances to private properties.

"Send new message to closest tablet," Hal commanded his mobile. He looked up at the grey sky, through his improvised umbrella and watched as the message lit-up the display. As if peering through a small window, he read:

New Message – received today at 9:17am
RE: Position of Triage Assessment Specialist at Pacific Insurance & Pharmacology of San Francisco.

Harold Dune MD, LFT:
Thank you for your interest in our PIP Laboratory in San Francisco. Unfortunately, while your credentials more than qualify you for the position, your unsponsored regional residency does not yet satisfy this company's hiring policies. Upon fulfilling a minimum residency requirement of six months, or obtaining a certified sponsorship, you are welcome to resubmit your résumé for consideration. Thank you for your interest.
Kestra Torres
Human Resources Manager

Unblinkingly Hal read through the message several more times, as if he expected the content to change. After a few minutes, suddenly conscious of what must be a peculiar stance, he lowered his arms and hoped the rain would wash away his disappointment. Once the collapsible tablet fell to his side, Hal's head was soaked in seconds.

He numbly began to wander down the sidewalk, dumbfounded at how something as trivial as an address or prominent signature would be reason enough to deny a qualified candidate even a simple interview.

Eventually, he noticed the scenery slowly changing as he stared at the street. He was thinking adamantly about two things: how are people who are not fortunate enough to be granted sponsorship able to make it in this town if they can't find work, and how is the street still so filthy after all this rain?

It was about then he realized that he was no longer on the sidewalk. Without time to decide which way to go, his attention was seized by the Doppler sound effects of reverse jets coming from a police cruiser in a desperate attempt to avoid adding him to the grungy roadway.

Jerked from his stupor, Hal clumsily leapt in the direction he was facing. The sleek vehicle narrowly missed his left leg by mere millimeters.

The silvery craft came to a stop. As the rush of wind its momentum created dissipated, the driver's mirrored window shifted to a tinted transparency and partially lowered to reveal a thirty-something Asian woman behind the controls. Her brown eyes, shadowed both by the car and the shiny black hair obstructing her face like an ancient soldier's helmet, projected a piercing glare of dour castigation.

"It must be your lucky day," she began. "If you're looking for a lift to the morgue then you stepped in front of the right vehicle. Do yourself a favor. If you're going to continue drifting around in the rain, either watch for traffic or look for crosswalk signals."

The window started to slide back up, but not before Hal received a look of what could be classified as pity, though he chose to presume it one of curiosity. The window returned to its mirrored appearance and the cruiser sped away uphill.

After the sobering effects of his near-death experience, Hal went in search of the nearest public transit stop. This wasn't the first time he failed to get a job, so he had no excuse for his disassociation. If Hal's upbringing and military training taught him anything, it was that setbacks should only strengthen his resolve. He knew he had to either find a way around his residency issue or locate employers who don't have the requirement.

Two: Missing and Unidentified Persons

Deputy Inspector Kimber Lee accelerated her police cruiser and attempted to refocus on the pending case at the medical examiner's office. Her eager-to-please counterpart from the San Francisco Police Department resumed the one-sided conversation he began when she picked him up.

"I wonder what that guy's problem was. Maybe it's the weather? Three days of this is enough to make almost anybody crazy. I hope this case isn't just another absconded geriatric person. We've been getting so many of those lately that I'm about to…"

"Jon, you're a reserve member of the Missing and Unidentified Persons Division. If the duties required aren't exciting enough for you then you might want to consider returning to your usual detail," Kimber interrupted.

"Yes, yes of course. Believe me it's crossed my mind. But don't you find it odd that the body we're going to see was transported here instead of remaining in the Food Belt where it was collected? It would be just as easy for you, or anyone from your office, to go there rather than shipping the body here. Seems like our friendly neighbors to the east are trying to pass the buck, don't you think?"

He makes a good point, Kimber thought. The situation did indeed seem suspicious, but she wasn't about to let this glorified weekend warrior know that she requested this assignment because of those strange circumstances.

"We'll soon find out," she assured. "Perhaps it's just a simple matter of resources this region has that the Agrarians don't. But if you want to take a page from them and keep your hands clean as well, be my guest," she finished with a wry smile.

A few silent minutes passed and Kimber secretly congratulated herself. Usually her comments only enticed more conversation out of Officer Jon Colquitt. This time he only peered out his window. To her wary surprise, he didn't utter another word for the rest of the trip.

They arrived at the civic parking area and allowed the automated parking attendant to shelve the cruiser as if it were seasonal decorations going into storage. Its robotic platforms effortlessly lifted the cruiser and stacked it high overhead, leaving little space between her car and the surrounding vehicles. The process was a bit of a novelty to Kimber compared to other regions she frequented that didn't yet use the contraption, so she savored the brief moment.

They made their way to the morgue to find the pathologist just getting started with the autopsy. The space was kept pristine; the usual look, smell, and feel of the average autopsy suite were mostly absent.

The normally mild olive skin tone of Dr. Mutara appeared shockingly dark in contrast to his white medical garb and stainless steel equipment. Kimber usually met with him after his work was concluded, to occasionally read between the lines of his autopsy report. He spotted the pair stepping through the second set of sterile atmospheric doors and hurried over to them like a maître d at an upscale restaurant.

"What'd we miss doc?" Jon asked in his best salty-cop voice, his first words in nearly twenty minutes. A new record, to be sure, Kimber mused.

"Forgive me for starting before you arrived but we've come across a few... anomalies with our friend's identification. I wanted to have some answers before you got here so I began the preliminary examination," the doctor said anxiously.

"What kind of anomalies?" Kimber asked, with a bit more excitement showing through than intended.

"Well, for starters, we've had to process each fingerprint individually. Running them all at once, which is standard procedure of course, has yielded some errors," Dr. Mutara replied. He seemed more calm as his poise returned; something the collected academic professional institutions around the world knew him for.

"Individually, we're getting a return of three distinct identities, and not aliases if that's what you're thinking. One identity appears more prominent, being found on four fingers, versus three each for the remaining two identities. Hardly enough evidence to satisfy either of our bosses I suspect. We also performed a dental and retinal scan with mixed results."

Like a skilled showman, the doctor paused briefly, both to allow the fusillade of confounding information to be processed, and to keep his audience in a state of suspense, starved for more information.

"Unfortunately, neither were of much help. All of his teeth have been replaced by a composite material, one that I understood to be primarily used for prosthetics in professional athletes and in Special Forces body armor, due mainly to its high cost and durability. This makes it an unreliable identifier. The retinal scan gave us a fourth identity in the right eye and an unrecorded source from the left."

"What about toe prints?" Inspector Lee wondered aloud. "There's a considerable database on those in this state; more so than the rest of the country anyway."

"Ah, brilliant" the doctor beamed as he raised his arms in disbelief for not having considered this already. He turned to request his autopsy assistant, known as a diener, to place the magnifier on the body's feet while everyone waited for the image to appear on the nearest monitor. A very close-up view appeared, and after reviewing the images for a few seconds Dr. Mutara furrowed his brow.

"That's odd." He walked over to the body to examine the feet himself, but judging by his perplexed sigh, his initial conclusion must've been confirmed.

"It seems our mysterious friend has had his friction ridges seared off in an apparent surgical manner. The edges are so clean I would have to remove the skin and study it more closely to tell you how it was even performed."

Aside from the hum of environmental fans and air purifiers, silence filled the room for a moment. Finally Jon broke the hiatus and asked, "So who is the prominent identity from the fingerprint return, and what did the guy die from?"

"Oh the cause of death was the easy part. Here we have the indicative burn from a perimeter drone," explained Dr. Mutara, gesturing to a deeply reddened mark about a dozen centimeters in diameter on the right side of the body's abdomen. "This nasty little wound on his oblique however, was the deathblow; by a bio-fletch no less."

"I'm sorry doc, but a what?" Jon asked thoroughly confused.

"Biological fléchette. It's basically a toxic dart that's made from organic byproducts of synthetic foods. It dissolves as it's absorbed by the body, leaving almost no trace of it except for the entry wound and contaminants in the system."

"Well then what's the point of having them if you can easily detect when they're used?"

"I asked that very same question the first time I came across one, detective. Simply identifying a bio-fletch wound, and the toxins it's composed of, which vary greatly by the way, is inadequate for homicide investigations, aside from determining cause of death, that is. It's practically impossible to trace its manufacturer and the particular delivery device used. It also makes determining time of death much more difficult depending on what they're made of."

The doctor paused briefly, gazing at nothing in particular, and then continued. "Bio-fletches are still fairly rare and expensive. Perhaps those factors will work in your favor in due time I should hope."

The room became silent again as Dr. Mutara went back to work and the two officers considered the discouraging information. Inspector Lee attempted to recall when and where she read about bio-fletches, but drew a blank. Then she realized one of Jon's questions wasn't addressed and redirected the doctor back to it.

"Oh yes, my apologies officers. The most frequently occurring identity from the fingerprint analysis belongs to none other than Doctor Miles Shepard."

Kimber shot an inquisitive glance at her partner but only got a shrug in reply. "Are we supposed to know who that is doctor?" Kimber asked, unconcerned about her obliviousness.

"Perhaps not, and please, call me Erwin. Miles Shepard practically pioneered the field of applied regenerative surgery, with a small group of other researchers of course."

Jon attempted to salvage their ignorance about the person and subject and asked, "You mean that new method of organ transplants?"

"It's much more complicated than transplantation I'm afraid, and it's over a decade old as well. With regenix, as it's referred to in medical circles, Dr. Shepard's team found a way to re-use almost any organ and tissue no matter the age or blood type of the donor or recipient; unless the age difference is too great or the organ has been compromised for one reason or another."

Shaking off the second round of failed medical trivia, Jon curtly replied, "That's all very interesting doc, but why are you so reluctant to identify this body as Shepard's?"

"Because his recorded date of birth would put him at 73 years of age. So far I've found nothing to make me think this person reached fifty. Now then, based on the nature of this already atypical situation, and the possibly high profile case it would be if this were indeed Miles Shepard, I'm going to have to ask you both to don a disposable clean suit for the remainder of this procedure."

~

The two returned to the gleaming autopsy room wearing the one-size-fits-all, white clean suit to find Dr. Mutara looking as befuddled over his patient as before. The baggy suit made a swishing sound with each movement. Wearing them always made Kimber wonder if this was how flying squirrels felt around ordinary squirrels.

Having already cut the 'Y' incision, the robotic arms that contained the laser scalpel, internal imaging probe, and a multitude of other instruments had receded back into their ceiling alcove. The body's chest cavity was exposed to the moderately larger world of the morgue.

The pristinely organized interior of the corpse was just as perplexing as its tanned and youthfully fit exterior. Prior to putting on the squirrel suit, she was prepared to proceed with investigating Dr. Shepard's apparent murder. Erwin's skepticism was however becoming infectious, and for good reason.

"Why does he look like a grade-school anatomy mannequin doc... sorry, Erwin?" she asked, putting into words what must've been on everyone's mind.

"A very good question inspector. I'm still uncertain as to whom this person is, but if he is indeed Dr. Shepard, it's clear he's become a product of his own design. I've never even heard of regenerative surgery this extensive. I don't think any of the major organs are original to this body."

"But that's a good thing in this case isn't it doc? Aren't these transplants cataloged and traceable?" Jon inquired hopefully, trying to regain some of the intellectual footing lost from earlier.

"Yes, that's correct detective, the legal ones are anyway," Erwin conceded. This last comment quickly wiped away the gratified look on Jon's face. "Whenever regenerative surgeries are performed, the transplanted organ is tagged with a chip that contains encoded data regarding: who the donor and recipient were, what was being donated, when the procedure took place, and where it occurred.

"The tags can only be read by certified instruments. We of course have the proper equipment to read the tags but it's only detecting five of them: two of which appear to have corrupted data, possibly due to the drone's stun bolt. Two others are obviously outdated; the listed recipients being female. The fifth one, however, at least gives us a little consistency. The donor is the same person identified from the right eye retinal scan -- Miles Shepard."

"So that's five sources saying this is Dr. Shepard." Jon interjected. "Is it safe to move forward under that assumption now and adapt the inquest if we come across conflicting evidence?"

"Only two sources I'm afraid, detective. Not near enough for a definitive identification given all the other factors. But I suppose it's as good a place to proceed as any. This examination will likely take longer than usual, so we can continue without you two if you'd prefer to take your leave. I'll keep you posted on any new developments," Dr. Mutara said without looking up from his patient.

Taking the hint from both gentlemen, Kimber motioned at Jon to go change, thanked Erwin, and took one last look at who they were calling Doctor Miles Shepard, for now anyway.

As Kimber changed out of her flying squirrel suit, her concern mounted. She'd only been on the case for a couple of hours and the unknowns were piling up much faster than the facts. She tried to pick a direction to head in with potential leads, but nothing useful came to her. She settled on seeking out an independent opinion, and fast before word of the decedent reached the media. Thankfully there was someone nearby who might be able to fit that bill.

THREE: EPIPHANY

Despite the weather continuing to be quite unforgiving, the hover bus was still busy for the mid-morning hour, so Hal resigned himself to stand for most of his ride home.

At Hal's stop, he descended the ramp and glanced around at the still mostly unfamiliar buildings at the corner of Union & Baker. The rain had subsided to a fine drizzle, but by the look of the cloud cover the heavier stuff could resume at any moment.

His spartan, one-bed/bath was a few blocks to the east of the Presidio. Several years ago, the trend of referring to objects more like a Brit would had caught on. Evidently San Francisco was the most European city in America, and this rebranding showed no sign of stopping anytime soon. Hal wasn't prepared to start calling his closet of an apartment a flat just yet, especially since his move there was only about four weeks ago. A time lapse that depressed him the more it crossed his mind, since he had little to show for it.

The front gate lock clicked open as the encrypted access code transmitted from his wrist mobile came into range of his building's proximity sensors. As Hal waited for the glossy, black metal security gate to allow passage into the building, he admired the once majestic design of the Victorian structure that still managed to peek through the garish, modern adaptations of the past few decades. A sigh managed to slip out due to his difference of opinion with the owner who conceded to such unthinkable renovations.

The wooden staircase creaked even than normal louder from all the moisture in the air, announcing to the entire building, and possibly the neighboring ones as well, that someone was ascending to the third floor. Hal's fellow housemates knew him as the out-of-work doctor from the south; some try to help him out by offering to pay for personal check-ups. He always respectfully declined as his lack of equipment didn't do anyone any good.

To Hal's astonishment, he was able to make it to his apartment without being interrogated by anyone and plop down into the heavily-used but still comfortable chaise lounge.

He was running low on funds, but if he tried to sell his chaise he'd likely only get enough for a meal or two out of it and wouldn't know what to do without it. It was still so relaxing he; tended to spend more time on it than any other piece of furniture, including his bed. His body knew this too. Within the short time he'd been lying down, his eyes automatically began to close. There was no time to sleep at the moment, but Hal saw no harm in indulging in a moment of peace to organize his thoughts.

After only a couple of minutes, he was snapped him out of his reverie by a fleeting memory. He examined the room to locate what might've made him so jumpy, and his eyes settled on the only decoration that hung on the wall. His military shadow box rested smartly on a sea of beige directly across from him, unconsciously beckoning his attention.

Two snakes twisted around a winged staff on the Corpsmen series of US Navy rating badges. The symbol had been somewhat of a theme for most of Hal's adult life. That caduceus on his patch became a catalyst for many discussions while in the service. Nobody in the Marine division he was assigned to even knew what a caduceus was, or its history. They merely recognized it as being associated with the medical field, along with crosses of assorted colors, or some amalgamation of those.

Hal smiled proudly as he recalled the several lessons in history, psychology, and even a little philosophy he gave to the laudable men and women he served with in those brutal conflicts of East Africa and Central Asia. The pride he felt was also somewhat bittersweet, because those who survived with their wits still intact could probably recite what he said during the precious few moments of downtime they had.

Being in combat was quite the ironic experience. The relentless training and readiness testing for those first learning their duties lasted several months. When finally feeling prepared and motivated about doing real missions, an extremely few number of people wanted to face combat ever again once it was all over. Focusing on the job and the bigger picture of the campaign sometimes helped to get through the worst of times, but the bond those who survive war acquire made it practically impossible to discuss what transpired with anyone not actually there.

All the awards and promotions in the world were meaningless when they were given for events that nobody wanted to have happen in the first place, and with results few expected to occur.

Unfortunately, this was a fairly accurate summary of Hal's combat career. He had been assigned to one of the best forward units in the US armed forces. He was fortunate to have risen through the ranks at a brisk pace. Yet everything seemed to change the day that anchors, indicating the rank of chief petty officer, were pinned to his uniform.

There were different expectations when someone became a Navy Chief. For one thing, everything a sailor knew, or thought he or she knew, was put to the test. All the work that had been done so frequently over the years, to the point of becoming routine, was taken away in lieu of managing a bunch of strangers to do the same tasks in different places while expected to maintain the same efficiency.

It was around this time Hal became disillusioned with the military. Separated from the Marines he served with, and instructing at the Naval Medical Center in San Diego with an endless supply of diffident corpsman, Hal couldn't imagine a more boring life compared to what he had been doing only a few months prior. He towed the line usually reserved for old salts who couldn't work in the field any longer, which certainly wasn't the case with him.

However, to both his relief and humility, others took notice of Hal's growing cynicism. He was eventually called to his commander's office one day, but he left that meeting a very different person.

Commander Scott Bowen was a down-to-business physician who spent most of his career working with infectious diseases the military had taken an interest in. Hal was still making his way into a chair across from the commander when an ultimatum was thrown his way; either find an open detail that might keep him in the Navy or consider seeking work in the private sector.

Hal opened his mouth to offer his resignation when Bowen asked two very candid questions that he'll never forget: "You have an undergraduate degree in criminology, isn't that right Chief?"

"Uh, yes sir," he managed to stumble out, having been caught a little off guard. "One of the reasons I joined was to help pay for that program, sir."

"I see. Well, what would you say to giving criminal investigation work a go with the Naval Criminal Investigative Service as a non-com?"

"I didn't think there were any more non-commissioned officers sir; not for the last couple decades at least," Hal responded dodging the question. "I was also under the impression that the NCIS hired civilians for their investigators."

"I can't speak for the other branches but the Navy still uses the warrant officer pay grades on occasion for temporary duty assignments. And, while the service primarily employs civvies, they still have a fair amount of active duty filling their ranks. This position isn't for an investigator per se, just assisting in investigative work."

"How temporary would this assignment be sir?"

"It's difficult to say, but I think it mainly depends on the person who takes the job. How well he or she is liked and if the work is a good fit, et cetera."

Hal tried to think of more questions to further stall answering the Commander's question, but none came to mind so he decided to do something extremely rare for him; follow his instincts.

"Well then, I suppose my answer is that I would very much enjoy trying my hand helping the NCIS sir."

"Excellent. You are ordered to report to building 120101, Camp Pendleton tomorrow at 0800, and are hereby advanced to the rank of Chief Warrant Officer 2 until further notice. Your official orders will be waiting for you there. Good luck Chief."

"Uh," Hal said expecting to hear some dreadful catch as he stood to shake Bowen's hand, "thank you sir."

By changing the venue of his stagnant career, the Navy was able to hold onto him for another three years. Although he was doing very little in the way of what a typical corpsman's duties were, Hal was back to working around Marines where he felt considerably more comfortable. Each day offered something new, as he provided medical and psychological expertise to a pair of agents in a variety of cases ranging from domestic violence to unnatural deaths.

Hal became so reliable and enthusiastic about this work that he was able to obtain a license as a forensic technician, which is recognized in over thirty states and in all military installations. He also did a fair amount of undercover work. It was on one of those missions Hal met a Marine officer who would later become his wife, Lindsey.

Damn she looked good in uniform! Hal recalled. She was a captain at the time, and Hal was posing as one undercover. Since she wasn't part of an open investigation he took a chance and told her who he really was. Lindsey and Hal had some off-the-radar fun for a while, but it didn't take him long to realize that she was a career officer through and through.

Realizing this, Hal understood that it would take a drastic overture to move the relationship to the next level. After nearly twelve years of active service, with 18 months in a semi-secret relationship with a senior officer, he decided to not renew his enlistment. This move afforded him the opportunity to both stay with Lindsey in the militarily-accepted manner and pursue a medical doctorate.

The MD program normally takes six years, to include residency, but Hal completed it in just over four, due to transferable credits and experience. During this time he and Lindsey married, and together had a son. Things were well for the three of them, but Hal's desire to expand his medical career quickly gained momentum. He broached the subject of moving upstate, where the medical fields were more abundant and paid far better. No matter how many times and how many ways he asked, the answer was still the same; Lindsey was happy with what she was doing and where she was doing it.

Suddenly, during the reminiscing of his active duty days, a switch flipped in his head. Hal had an epiphany that caused him to bolt up out of his seat and he berated himself for not thinking of it before. He knew of an employer who was almost always hiring medical professionals. He doubted they had residency requirements since it was a federal agency; the Veterans Administration. As fate would have it, the VA Hospital at Fort Miley was only a couple miles away.

Hal hastily went searching for his computer. During his month of living in the city, he relied mainly on his mobile and flex-tablet. He didn't think he'd even taken his desktop out of the box yet. He found it in the bedroom still waiting to be unpacked. He placed the shoe-sized device near a wireless power terminal, and waited for it to orient itself while he manipulated its holographic display.

Just as he began to search for the VA's contact information, his mobile informed him about an incoming call from his son. Hal verbally directed it to transfer the call to his computer and instantly saw the eager face of his six year-old.

"Hi Sean! It's good to see you!"

"Hey dad! Did you get the job?"

He had to ask didn't he? "No son, I'm sorry to say I didn't. I haven't lived here long enough to work in most places, it turns out, but there's still plenty more to try."

"I know you won't give up dad, you never do."

So young but he learns quickly, Hal thought. Very little ever got by Sean unnoticed; both his parents were the same way.

"Still haven't unpacked yet dad? I don't see any of the pictures I sent you."

Hal smiled, imagining Sean using some of that extra-sensory perception he just parsed. "Slowly but surely Sean. I haven't had any guests to impress yet."

"Well the sooner you get a job and your... flat? Is that what they call it there? As soon as you're ready, I can come and visit!"

"And that's the best motivation I can get," he said with a grin so large it warmed his whole face.

"Well I guess I'll let you get back to work, at finding work. I love you dad!"

"I love you too Sean. I'll see you soon." They disconnected and Hal stared for a few moments longer at the empty space where his son's image was just projected. Remembering what he needed to do to bring Sean there physically, Hal got to task, just like the boy told him to.

Four: Bread Crumbs

Inspector Lee piloted her cruiser more leisurely than she had on the way to the morgue as she took Jon back to his office and tried to assemble a plan for the inquest. He'd been quiet since they shed their lab suits, so she kept her fingers crossed that chatting a little about the case wouldn't open the floodgates.

"You look deep in thought Jon. Care to share what's on your mind, or would you like me to guess? I'm probably just as confused by this guy as you are."

"Good guess but I was actually thinking about my behavior in the morgue. I can't help but feel a little embarrassed about how I acted there."

Kimber gave him a look of utter disbelief. She wasn't sure if it was due to the absurdity of his claim or that it was a topic she never would've predicted.

"Don't take this the wrong way but that's ridiculous. I've worked with Dr. Mutara on a lot of cases and I know that he doesn't like it when there are still mysteries with his findings. And I'm sure he downright despises it when he suspects another doctor of ethics violation or fraud. There are a number of factors about this that we've not come across before, so he's just getting irritated with the situation. I wouldn't give it a second thought."

"There's some logic to that I suppose," he finally responds after a minute of silence. "Perhaps it's just my lack of familiarity with him."

Here he goes again over-thinking things just explained to him, Kimber brooded, wondering if it was perhaps a defense mechanism. "Good to hear, because there's too much we don't know with this case and I would like you to focus on that instead. I need you to dig up as much as you can on Miles Shepard, as well as the other names identified at the morgue. I'm going to drop you off but I'll be back after I run an errand, if you need me to. There's an informant I'd like to pay a visit to. Getting him to talk one-on-one is difficult enough, so adding a second person to the mix will make it damn near impossible."

"I can do the research in transit if you need me nearby for backup. I'll wait in the car or a nearby hotspot," Jon posed, starting to perk up a bit.

Kimber considered the idea. It would save her a trip if she needed to act fast, but she concluded he would concentrate better at his office workstation.

"Thanks for the concern but to avoid detection, of you, I'd have to park far enough away that it would defeat the purpose of back-up. I also may have a few other stops to make depending on the quality and quantity of information I get. Besides, you probably have other duties that might require your... special kind of attention."

Jon slowly turned to face her and cracked an incredulously sarcastic grin to ask, "And what, Inspector Lee, does that mean exactly?"

"Oh nothing. Just checking to see if you actually did any work when I'm not around. Thank you for not forcing me to bring it up with your lieutenant," she said matching his smile.

"She wouldn't know my day-to-day anyway," Jon replied, eyeing Kimber indignantly. "In any case, message me if you need anything or change your mind about back-up. Don't make me come looking for you," he finished with pseudo-sternness, trying to look as serious as he could manage.

"Thanks for the warning. I shouldn't be too long but you never know with these things. They're sometimes difficult to gauge. I'll keep you in the loop, don't worry."

~

Kimber let out a sigh of relief as she departed the SF Police Academy on Amber Street and headed eastward across town once again, to what was left of the retired naval shipyard known as Hunters Point. Jon carried the rank of sergeant and was considered a detective, but much of his time was spent doing research the department depended on to assess various police programs, and comparing it to others throughout the state. Since he typically didn't operate in the field, the Academy begrudgingly granted him some workspace, provided he supported academy affairs when called upon.

Though he's no savant, he frequently consulted his peers in their casework by creating innovative ways to solve obstinate inquests, when conventional investigative techniques fail. Even with this rare vitae, Jon's eagerness to return to fieldwork is the primary rationale behind the brass permitting him to assist on what was deemed to be low-priority cases; such as most that are within the MUP's jurisdiction.

The semi-new facilities on Hunters Point came into view and Inspector Lee continued to mentally prepare herself for meeting with an informant she hadn't contacted in at least a year.

The old naval shipyard became a veritable island due to severe floods and earthquakes of decades past. The only access point from the city connects to the facility by a detachable bridge with guard gates on each end. Many of the buildings and large dock equipment that remained were upgraded by the Coast Guard when they took over the property some twenty years prior; after they absorbed a couple other federal agencies resulting in a boost in their formerly deteriorating budget.

There were unsubstantiated reports that the flooding which enveloped the Bay Area was quite the respite for the coasties; which abbreviated the base's costly refurbishment considerably. Before the sale to the USCG, it spent time as a provisional disposal center for hazardous contraband seized by the Departments of Agriculture and Energy.

Kimber veered her attention back to the imminent reunion once again. She considered informants to be a bit of an enigma in the law enforcement community; those who didn't have one often wished they did, and many who handled one or more knew not to get attached because most didn't last long. Some were even eager to rid themselves of the responsibility since their reliability was too tenuous.

Interventions with them were only when absolutely necessary, not only because of the hassle of pulling them out of whatever hole he or she had gotten into, but also because the information provided was entirely circumspect. Their reports could be completely fabricated and verifying their validity could take more time than what they were worth.

This particular source was an intelligence analyst for the Coast Guard. Since they had taken on a slew of other duties for Homeland Security, a lot of information headed their way. That was one of the expedient points about government; if one agency came under fire for one reason or another, such as the National Security Agency in the early 2000s, some of their questionable endeavors were simply redirected into another agency.

As Kimber approached the first guard gate, her trepidation about whether or not the information she brought to trade was sufficient caused her lower back to perspire, which quickly became an annoying itch. If she scratched now however, it may send the wrong message to the assault-rifle carrying guard.

"Inspector Lee to see Analyst Martin Tucker; I don't have an appointment," she announced as she extended her arm to the portable identity scanner.

The guard vigilantly shifted his eyes from the scanner's display to Kimber as the results appeared. He then excused himself to his booth and was overheard using the radio. When he left her view, Kimber tried to scratch her back as inconspicuously as she could but relief eluded her. The guard stepped back out just as she started to make some progress.

"Please park in the visitor lot off Nimitz Avenue on your right as you exit the crossing. Analyst Tucker will meet you there ma'am," the guard instructed. The opaque, ocean blue gate blocking her path slowly opened and the guard stood in a distinguished stance next to her cruiser. Kimber took one last look at the neatly pressed, dark-blue uniform with gleaming equipment on the utility belt before applying the accelerator a bit more firmly than she intended.

It was a short drive to the small visitor lot, since Hunters Point was about half the size it used to be. Kimber doubted the base entertained many visitors, so the four-space lot kept close to the interior guard was in pristine condition.

Kimber spied Marty hurrying out from behind a nearby building toward where she parked. His dark, slender form offset by the light-grey buildings moved with purpose but with the grace of a newborn giraffe. He reached the cruiser a little out of breath with either an angry or panicked look in his eyes; Kimber couldn't tell which.

"What in holy hell are you doing here?" he demanded as Kimber closed her door. "I was hoping you had forgotten about me so we could both move on with our lives."

"Forget about you? How could I possibly do that? I was just waiting until you thought I did, while you built up your comfort zone," she answered with a wry smile.

"You think it's funny that you just roll up here any time you please and try to get classified information from me? I'll probably get questioned for a week after this little conjugal visit!"

"Whoa, calm down Marty. I never said anything about classified information. I know it's been a while but you know damn well that I don't ask for things that could get us both in trouble; not without something mutually beneficial anyway."

"Calm down? That's easy for you to say. You don't have anyone to hurt but yourself if you get fired or arrested. I get regular security clearance checks here and have a family, or have you forgotten that people depend on me?"

Kimber stared at him and tried to think of a reply that didn't involve breaking his nose. She then reminded herself that she needed him at the moment and tried to ignore Marty's jab at the two lowest points in her life; a miscarriage and subsequent divorce that alienated her from both her biological and extended families.

"I know you're pissed at me right now but don't make this personal. I can go there too if you'd like, but I need some help on a case and I doubt I'll find many useful answers through the regular channels, with some semblance of discretion anyway."

"Does this, by chance, have something to do with the unidentified body found on the perimeter of the Realignment and Agrarian Regions?"

Kimber blinked at Marty, and disregarded the notion of asking how he'd heard about that already. With the amount of data coming through this base, and the fact that Marty really was one of the best in this field she'd ever met, she tried to hide her amazement.

"Why yes, as a matter of fact it does. There's still a lot we don't know but he was killed by a bio-fletch. Who has access to weapons like that?"

"A bio-fletch? That's incredible! I can't tell you the last time I've even heard someone mention one of those," Marty gushed with excitement, replacing his ire of a few seconds ago.

"So its rare usage should make it easy to track right?" Kimber prodded with some hopefulness in her tone.

"Not really, no. Only a few companies manufacture them. It tends to change based on the annually renewed contracts for bio-weapons, since the darts themselves are made from synthetic byproducts. Also, client lists are usually kept strictly confidential. The best way to track bio-fletches is to find out who uses the devices that can fire one. The problem however lies in that fact that most of them are designed to function with a wide-array of cartridges, including the bio-fletch of course."

"So you're telling me, going this route can't be done?"

"I know what you're trying to do you know. It may work this time but that's only because I'm interested myself. Searching for someone who might have procured bio-fletches will be a waste of time, but I'll see what I can do about getting you a list of those using the equipment. If this is all you have to go on though, you're going to find yourself out of leads very soon."

Kimber fought and failed to hide her grin. She'd used the same tactic on Marty many times without a peep from him, until now. "Thanks Marty, you're a lifesaver. It's funny you mention other leads because I'm curious what you know about regenerative surgery. Is there a demand for it in the black market, or anywhere outside the conventional outlets?"

Marty gave her a look of utter disbelief. "There's a demand for almost everything of value in the black market, and anything in the regen field is a hot item, both legal and not. Hell, I could be the guy who makes the transplant appointments and still be able to retire in a third of the time I could with this job. Some people would literally sell their soul to extend their life even a little for something as trivial as bragging rights. Regenerative surgery is one of those concepts that might actually allow those rich enough to live forever."

"Yes of course, but hypothetically, if someone has the money for the procedure why would he or she bypass state and federal law by going under the table to transplant organs without the proper tags when a simple DNA comparison will show the discrepancy?"

"Wow," Marty responded aghast. "The body from the Food Belt had untagged organs?"

"I didn't stay for the whole autopsy but last word was probably all the organs were from someone else, or multiple someone elses. More than half of which had unreadable or outmoded tags for each pieces."

Marty nodded thoughtfully, then, as if waking from a deep trance asked, "so who did the organs with readable and functioning tags identify as the recipient?"

"A few different people actually. But you still haven't answered my question."

"Oh, well, the elites are gonna do what they do regardless, as you're fully aware," Marty added in a patronizing tone as another dig at her former in-laws. Kimber aimed a contemptuous glare his direction, prompting him to continue.

"However, receiving an organ is only half the process. From what I understand, you're not going to know if the organ came from where you were told it did unless you have a fondness for transparency, and I'd wager most don't; particularly those who try to hide their identity like your friend apparently did."

"Sure, sure, but I imagine those donor lists are lengthy, so again, if someone has the money I don't understand the necessity of going underground to get it done."

"You can't possibly be that naïve. Even after all these years of working together. There may be a long list of donors, but depending on the organ, the donor typically has to be dead. I assure you the demand is *much* greater than the supply. Why do you think the state approved a division that exclusively investigates missing persons?"

It was a question Kimber had wondered on many occasions but she couldn't say she considered it in this context. Thinking back over the six years since she was assigned to the MUP, when it was still an emergent division of the state police, if memory served her a significant number of cases involved either an elderly or transient person.

Kimber's train of thought was interrupted when she noticed Marty's hand waving in her face.

"Hello? Did I lose you with that one?" he asked with a content smirk. "Alright come clean, whose body turned up in the snow? You know how this works. If you want my help its quid pro quo and so far it's been pretty one-sided."

Inspector Lee slumped against her cruiser resignedly, desperately hoping he bought the answer she was about to divulge because she really did need his assistance. "We don't have a strong confirmation yet, but based on four fingerprints and one or two of the organ tags we are currently deeming the body to be that of Doctor Miles Shepard."

"The man himself," Marty murmured. "You only have the prints and a couple tags linked to Shepard? What about all the biometric identifiers, and DNA?"

"We're following up with a few leads but it's mostly inconclusive until the full autopsy report is in. When I left the morgue that's all we had. So are you going to help me or not?"

"I'm not sure how I can. You haven't given me much to go on," he responded defensively.

"Well, to start, find out what you can about who is using bio-fletch gear in those regions. And if you're up for it, see if you can't give me a name of someone who works in the regen black market around here."

"The bio-fletch angle might take some time, for the reasons I explained earlier, but the latter request I can help you with right now. He was a VA employee suspected to be involved with the market but they fired him on the accusation alone. You know how government works. I think he still lives in town. His name is Aramis Navoa. He shouldn't be too difficult to locate."

"I think I can remember that name," Kimber said dryly. "If there wasn't enough evidence to charge him before how do you know he was guilty, or if he's even still involved that he would know anything helpful?"

"I didn't say he would be helpful. But I base that on the fact he was still able to stay afloat in this city as a homeless outreach specialist with the VA, in Pacific Heights no less. All that despite his highly publicized trial due to several clients turning up missing, as well as multiple audits for tax evasion. To me that says something is amiss."

"Seems like you've taken a special interest in the guy. Why have you devoted so many of your precious brainwaves to him?"

"There used to be a lot of homeless in San Francisco, many of them veterans, and some of them were my mates. I'd be very interested to know what happened to them and the rest of the transient population in the city who weren't forced into retirement centers."

"I see. I'll let you know if I find anything. You know how to reach me about the bio-fletches." Kimber returned to her DeLorean Motor Company police cruiser and gave Marty an imperious salute as she steered toward the bridge. He responded with a genial shake of the fist and was lost in the foggy blue security wall a few seconds later.

Five: Connecting Dots

Kimber departed the Coast Guard Station at Hunter's Point in a hurry. She was relieved to enlist Marty's help, but still wasn't comfortable with how much he knew about her personal life, and the ease with which he pushed her buttons.

Not many people knew Kimber's history and she made a concerted effort to keep it that way. Too many already knew even a few of the details, but Marty knew most of it through their many contacts, and he didn't let her forget that for a moment.

There were of course rumors floating around about her at the various police departments and federal agency field offices she frequently partnered with, as was customary in the world of law enforcement. The truth was far more devastating however than any rumor she'd heard, at least to her.

Kimber had so many regrets in life that she would be hard-pressed to pick one, or even a couple, that could be overlooked. She had barely finished her degree in criminology when she married her college boyfriend; under pressure from both their parents. He was from a somewhat wealthy Japanese-American family and her family saw little future with a criminology degree.

The wedding was just past the two-year anniversary of their first date but it still felt like a whirlwind. The honeymoon seemed to last nearly the entire first year. All they did was travel; mostly to accompany her new husband on business trips, but there were occasional jaunts for recreation as well.

The excitement of visiting new places began to wear off as the loneliness and boredom of spending more time alone than together became the norm. Pleading with Robyn to cut a meeting short here or extend a lunch there to no avail only revealed that his family's business meant more to him than she did.

Instead of giving in to the role of a demure housewife, Kimber decided to look for a job where she could use the degree she worked hard to earn, much to the objection of both families. Her own parents wanted her to get pregnant as soon as possible, and Robyn's parents saw no reason for anyone in their family to seek employment outside of their firmware company.

Rob, on the other hand, was appreciatively supportive. So much so that he helped connect her with the state's Board of Inspectors, a state managed organization that was federally mandated and funded.

Six grueling months later, Kimber graduated from the Inspector Academy third in her class. She was assigned to the Threats to Regional Sovereignty Division and was excited to be starting her first job. Unfortunately, the foreign taste of independence was cut short by an unexpected pregnancy.

Becoming pregnant wasn't the unfortunate part per sé; it was the timing of the whole thing. Kimber was thrilled to apply the degree she had invested so much in, and felt fulfilled in challenging herself more than she had the previous 18 months. She was crestfallen to not maintain that position for a full year before she was ordered to go on limited duty. Limited duty, regarding pregnancy, meant being taken off field work to do administrative or other support duties until at least a month after giving birth.

Everyone in her family was ecstatic except her. Robyn could sense Kimber's despair but was pleased none-the-less. A tragic accident however, would change things forever.

On Inspector Lee's final field mission, the light transport she and three colleagues were traveling in lost altitude and crashed in the Sierra Mountains. One of the four died, another never walked again on his own biological legs, and Kimber lost the child and damaged her uterus enough that hoping for any future of motherhood was "highly unlikely." Her family was quick to close the proverbial door on her. Robyn was the only person to visit her in the hospital, but he avoided the topic of children altogether.

Recovery was slow. The constant reminders that nobody in her family wanted Kimber in law enforcement to begin with made it intolerable though. The final straw with her husband's parents was when Kimber announced her intentions to return to work. The response started with utter disbelief, and then quickly proliferated into outright belligerence.

Within two weeks back on the job, Kimber was served with divorce papers by Robyn's family attorney. She could tell Rob was deeply conflicted about the matter. In not so many words he explained that his parents had threatened to cut him off if he continued staying with her. He acquiesced to those demands and their marriage was annulled after only two years to the day; making four years for their entire courtship.

The Lee family was equally unforgiving. They maintained that, in their mind, Kimber destroyed her best chance at a prosperous future. The conciliatory exchanges that followed essentially resulted in her being disowned. Kimber would occasionally send them assorted missives, for holidays and other celebrated events, but received nothing in return.

To both her surprise and bewilderment, the only person from the disaster of her past who maintained any contact at all was Robyn. He had since remarried to the perfect woman, in his parents' eyes, and had two beautiful children.

Kimber's unwelcome trip down misery lane was thankfully interrupted by the friendly sound from a police network alert. The fact that any number of terrible things that could be going on in the state right now was announced by happy tunes had long been a source of amusement for her.

"This is Lee, what do you have Jon?"

A faint image of the detective, presumably sitting at his workstation, materialized at the center of her windshield. This location was selected to give attention to the message while not distract the driver so much as to cause a collision.

"Came across some interesting stuff actually. Where are you heading? I'd like to estimate how much time I have," Jon answered somewhat cautiously.

"I haven't decided yet, but that's likely to change depending on what you've learned."

"Uh, ok. Well the doc contacted me with an updated donor list, and the ones I've tracked down so far have confirmed deaths of at least two years ago. He's also obtained a DNA sample of what he assures me is the primary host, but has had no luck verifying him as Shepard. His physician won't release that information without either a death certificate or court order. I contacted Shepard's office to inquire on his whereabouts and was told he was on a promotional skiing trip somewhere upstate and wouldn't be back for a few days."

Kimber sighed, hoping desperately that this was a simple misunderstanding and not some corporate cover-up. It's not uncommon with MUP cases, or inquests in general, that a lot can change even after only a few hours. Protocol dictates being prepared for changes or at least control how they're handled.

"That doesn't really give us much Jon, other than keeping the focus on Shepard. Got anything else?"

"Yes, I do," Jon responded with a bit more vigor. "I was doing some digging on Shepard, and while there's a trove of articles on him I found evidence of tampering with the search results; both deletion and strategic editing of public records within the last twelve hours."

Oh great Kimber thought. The prospect of a cover-up just went from notion to probability. "Were you able to find a source or get any clue as to what was targeted?"

"No sources yet but whomever is behind it has thus far been very careful, as you might imagine. He, she, or they appear to still be at it, so I activated several sensor bots and planted them on articles most likely to be altered to try and catch them in the act."

Kimber started to get into some late-morning traffic, so she paused a few seconds in thought. "Wait, how do you know which articles are more likely to get attention from these people? What are they trying to undo exactly?"

Jon smiled again, pleased that the inspector was paying at least *some* attention to what he was saying. "I'm not entirely sure, but based on the targeted articles I've found the discrepancies appear to be isolated around some dissension Shepard's been forming toward his own company over the years."

Trying to clean him up to make him match the poster-boy image he's been given no doubt, Kimber mused. "Ok, good work; keep me posted on our digital ghost. I have another request while I have you on the line. Can you give me a location and any pertinent information on an Aramis Navoa?"

"Sure thing. Is this any relation to this case?"

"I'll let you know if he turns out to be of any use," Kimber snapped. "What can you tell me about him?"

Jon awkwardly cleared his throat as he mentally summarized the data that glowed in front of him. "Ok, former VA employee, let go seven years ago for suspected fraud, kidnapping, and conspiracy. Charges were dropped due to lack of evidence but not until after the IRS had a field day with his finances. He was never arrested but ended up paying almost a million bucks in fines. Current address puts him at an upscale apartment building on Steiner Street adjacent to Alta Plaza Park."

Jon took a deep breath before asking his next question, aware of his penchant for saying the wrong things to the inspector at the wrong times, according to her. "Are you planning on paying this guy a visit?"

"I was thinking about it. Do you have any other leads to go on since this one is already reaching?"

"Oh, I didn't know he was a lead," Jon countered more brazenly than he intended. "My sensor bots haven't given me a hit yet but I asked because the State Licensing Bureau has him at over two full meters tall and 135 kilos. Since you had me look him up I'm guessing you don't know the guy, and judging by his file pic you may want some help dealing with him. I am your partner on this after all."

Kimber wanted to tell Jon to back off and not get any more involved. She worked alone more often than not and was not only used to the autonomy, but her office mates stopped requesting to collaborate with her years ago. Jon was absolutely right though. She didn't know how Mr. Navoa would react, or even how to explain why she was knocking on his door. She hated to admit it, but she needed his help. However, she wasn't yet prepared to reveal how the info came about.

"Good point. Transfer his file to my cruiser and I'll pick you up on my way to Pacific

Heights. Thanks for lookin' out Jon." Inspector Lee saw a victorious smile on his face before the windshield returned back to normal. Kimber made a turn to put her on course to retrieve Jon. The new route was less busy so she began to work on a cover story so Navoa wouldn't immediately call his lawyer before they were face-to-face.

~

The ride over to Alta Plaza Park was spent learning everything they could about Aramis Navoa. He was a Samoan, which might explain his large frame. Despite his tax troubles and lack of work, being able to remain in his expensive flat was a mystery to both the IRS and housing authority.

Jon was strangely quiet since Kimber collected him from his office at the Police Academy. There were a few times where he looked like he might say something but then decided against it; presumably still trying to figure out how she came across Navoa's name and didn't know how to broach the subject a second time, she presumed.

Kimber was also trying to think of ways to get Navoa to talk without making shallow threats that clearly wouldn't affect him after all he'd been through. After some internal to and fro, she decided to confide in Jon because they were short on time and she was running low on ideas.

"Jon, it's not really fair to bring you into a situation without knowing at least a little about what brought us here, so I'll fill you in as much as I can without compromising anyone. I got Navoa's name from my informant when I asked if he, or she, knew of someone in the black market for regenerative surgery. The problem this raises now though is..."

"How we approach him without tipping off the fact that legally we shouldn't be talking to him about this in the first place?" Jon cut in. "I thought you'd never ask," he added with an impatient grin. "Luckily, I continued researching him after we disconnected and have an idea that may at least get him talking about *something*."

Kimber let out a faint sigh of relief, and hoped Jon didn't notice. Even though she was coming up empty on a plan herself, she was skeptical of his before he even described it, for reasons that were unclear to her. She asked him to elaborate while making a mental note to work on her pessimism.

"I don't think Navoa leaves his place very often because he averages between 15 to 18 hours a day on the net; unless he just signs on to an active account and walks away to give anyone watching that impression. Anyway, I was thinking we could fake our way in by accusing him of trying to buy regulated equipment, or something, and then let him off the hook by concluding that his account was hacked."

Kimber couldn't help staring agape at him. "That's brilliant Jon! Better than anything I could come up with. But if he really is on that much wouldn't he have a system to support it, like high-end malware or some such?"

"Anything is possible with this sort of thing, but as far as I can tell his system is pretty standard. Keep in mind though that I consider myself only slightly above average in this particular field, otherwise I'd probably be doing forensic tech work instead."

"Well, from what we've read on Navoa, there's been little indication he's any better off than that in terms of concealing his online behaviors. Whatever we do will be improvised anyway, so we might as well go for it."

"Ok," Jon said emphatically. "So what are we actually going to press him on then?"

Six: Misdirection

The sleek cruiser came to a quiet stop in front of Navoa's ivory, twelve-story building. Ever since the city restricted street parking in residential areas of San Francisco several years ago, the streets were a lot cleaner and clearer. Naturally however, government vehicles were authorized to park almost anywhere during normal work hours, or emergencies.

This policy came not long after the state began to limit the use of personal vehicles within urban areas, which was preceded by the invention of ROMES, or retrograde magnetic emitters. ROMES gave cars the ability to hover, and allowed some designs strictly regulated flight capability.

The pair's encrypted police proximity transmitter allowed them access into the apartment building, but they'd have to get into Navoa's flat the old-fashioned way; convince him to let them in. They rode the lift to the tenth floor and were amazed at its cleanliness. The lift car had spotless granite-looking panels kept in place by a dark pine molding; as striking a contrast as there ever was one, Kimber thought.

They exited the lift after only a few seconds and located Navoa's flat, number 1010. "Wow, they don't make 'em like they used to, do they?" Jon quipped before activating the intercom.

"Just a moment please," a strangely soothing voice answered through the hidden speaker of the intercom. The next time the voice was heard it still sounded pleasant but obvious irritation could be detected. "Identify yourselves please."

"Inspector Lee of the Governor's Bureau, and Detective Colquitt with SFPD, mister Navoa. We need to ask you a few questions."

Multiple locking mechanisms were undone and the door opened to a giant, hulk of a man wearing what could be described as bright loungewear. He was staring at them with utter disdain.

"I don't mean to be rude but I don't think it's possible for the police to have any more questions for me. You've already asked them all several times over."

"We're not here about that mister Navoa," Kimber replied matter-of-factly. "We're curious about your recent attempts to purchase restricted medical equipment."

Aramis stood frozen in the doorway like a mannequin for a moment before responding. "My apologies, I thought you might provide more information than 'restricted medical equipment' without my needing to ask. I've been under the police's magnifying glass for seven years. I'm afraid to even jaywalk. Do you really think I'm going to try something as silly as that?"

"Look Navoa," Jon interjected, "whether it makes sense or not, the attempted purchases were traced to this address, so there's either something illegal going on here or somebody's hacked your accounts and stolen your identity. Wouldn't at least one of these allegations be slightly concerning to you?"

The large man stood motionless for another moment, then, almost gracefully, side-stepped and gestured for the two officers to come in with his proportionally enormous arm. They walked down a short hallway, passed an impressive-looking, though quaint, kitchen on the left. The space then opened up to a well-decorated living room filled with antique tables and a wide array of art hanging from the walls and populating most of the horizontal surfaces.

Despite the good taste he had in wall adornments, it was clear Navoa hadn't used an interior decorator because the rest of the furniture, namely the chairs, were all of modern design, and cheaply made at that, except one heavily broken-in armchair.

There were also large windows at the other end of the room, which when weather permitted offered a phenomenal view of the city northbound. A small, guest bathroom faced opposite the windows with the entrance to the bedroom located on its right.

"Please, have a seat and tell me what I've allegedly tried to buy, and why I'd want such things in the first place," Aramis said in a manner that could settle an indignant child.

"Well Aramís... may I call you that?" Jon asked in his best sardonic tone not pronouncing the 's'.

"Actually no. My heritage isn't French and I wasn't named after a musketeer, so the 's' is meant to be emphasized."

"Thanks for the correction," Jon continued as he opened his folding tablet. "The items in question were various volumes of Tesynol, portable incubation containers, and other miscellaneous materials that aid in the regeneration of tissue."

"So you see why tracing these attempted purchases to you might raise some flags mister Navoa," Kimber cut in.

Aramis scoffed and shook his head. "Even if I were dumb enough to procure these items, how and where would I get an opportunity to use them? I am practically under lock and key here. I rarely leave, and you've undoubtedly noticed those chairs have hardly been used because I never have guests."

Kimber glanced over at Jon as he only just realized how new his chair appeared, in a less-than subtle way. She attempted to cover the oversight up by keeping Navoa on topic.

"We did notice mister Navoa. Why is it you rarely leave or have visitors? Since you're likely well-versed in double-jeopardy, there's no harm in explaining why you would have no use for those materials, or not be collaborating with individuals who do."

Aramis held a brief but steady gaze at the inspector, then to her partner, and then let out a deep sigh that seemed to deflate his composure some.

"I wasn't technically acquitted on some of the more serious charges, so double-jeopardy doesn't apply to me on what matters. I got the impression the judge simply got tired of seeing me, and the feeling was mutual. My legal team was genuinely quite good. The best money can buy. Unfortunately it wasn't my money that bought them, so as a sort of penance they essentially put me under house arrest, for both their protection and mine. In that order. They arrange for all my food and what-not to be delivered; for life if I understood them correctly."

"What made this legal team so special? Why would someone else pay them to represent you?" Jon asked truly curious.

"They were the VA's legal team, as far as the court was concerned. But unofficially they were proxies hired by bio-tech executives, and even regional governors on occasion."

"Ok, that's one question answered, how about the second? Why would the same organization who filed the charges against you also pay some hired guns to defend you?"

"Surprisingly enough, that's the first time I've personally been asked that question. As you may already know, the VA has been privately owned for over a decade. It's still managed by the government, but its funding comes from the same bio-tech conglomerate my lawyers sprang from. This is where the inconsistency originates; the charges were from one party and the defense from the other. As to why I was given a crack-team of lawyers is anyone's guess," Aramis explained nonchalantly, as if waiving off some invisible pest.

Kimber could see the ire mounting on Jon's face. Everyone in the room knew why he was given that legal team, despite not remembering the VA's change of benefactors. Navoa was still protective of his legal history, but he was clearly depressed about his livelihood, or lack thereof. She decided to press that issue to its breaking point.

"What would happen if you left mister Navoa?"

"Left? This flat? My life would surely be over, if not physically then in all the other existential ways the average person requires, or presumes, to continue surviving."

"Other than the material things, and vague threats, what's keeping you here, specifically? Moving somewhere you are not as well-known seems like a simpler solution, to both sides."

For the first time since they arrived, Kimber could see unmistakable fear in Navoa's round face. The kind of terror that keeps a giant, well-spoken man trapped in his own home for years. He certainly knew more than he'd been letting on but it was evident he had resigned himself to this fate.

"I assure you, inspector, that I have raised that point, amongst several others, many times to no avail. And their threats were far from vague."

Jon sat back in his chair in a huff, unable to tolerate Navoa's stonewalling any longer. "So instead of outing the people who have essentially ruined your life, you choose to be their patsy until you die or do something stupid? What kind of life is that? We came here to investigate attempts to obtain controlled equipment but the real crime here seems to be blackmail and conspiracy!"

Aramis dabbed his now soaked brow with a stylish handkerchief and nervously shook his head. "I appreciate what you're trying to do but it's not quite that simple. Kes personally told me that they were waiting for the statute of limitations..."

Navoa's words were cut short by an explosion from the large windows behind him. A projectile of intense heat and light blasted through the pressurized outer window, seared its way through his chair and upper torso, and then shot past Kimber on the right to easily bore its way through the wall that led to the bedroom.

The officers were up in a flash; weapons drawn and finding cover, Jon to the kitchen and Kimber in the guest bathroom, while also trying to find the source of the attack. The forlorn, excessively decorated flat was now covered with glass and carried the ozone scent of burnt flesh.

As Kimber's adrenaline began to dissipate, reducing the pounding of her heart so she could actually hear what was going on, she noticed the unmistakable whistling sound of Dyson blowers coming from the window.

Quick movement from Jon on her left grabbed her attention instantly. Her eyes widened as the restrained fear edging through his facial expression materialized into recognition in her mind as he simultaneously mouthed the words "bird of prey drone." Realizing the high likelihood that the drone had sophisticated targeting scanners, Kimber looked back at Jon hoping he had some miracle strategy.

The normally enigmatic detective made a cross sign with his hands, indicating he proposed starting a cross fire, with the collected confidence of a combat veteran. He took a deep breath, to help further calm himself, and began a countdown from three with his fingers.

When the countdown ended, the pair emerged from their individual defensive positions. Both searched for a visual on their quarry. Sound from the drone's fans directed Jon's gaze toward the ceiling and he spotted it hovering next to an opalescent ceiling fixture. He took aim with his Selective-Variable-Repeater, and gasped in terror as he heard the drone readying another magnesium round in its magnetic-accelerator cannon. The drone's canon was pointed squarely at Kimber, who had yet to acquire her target.

"To me!" Jon yelled, startling his partner into diving in his direction as a streak of blinding white light tore past where she stood mere seconds prior.

Kimber rolled toward the center of the room, forcing the drone to change its position. Jon tried to draw its fire by abandoning his refuge behind the fridge. He dashed over the counter, through an opening that led from the kitchen to the dining area, but the counter wasn't as smooth as he estimated.

The drone took the bait. It effortlessly drifted backwards, remaining close to the ceiling, and began to target Jon as he struggled to make it over the serving bar.

Kimber saw her opportunity to end the cat-and-mouse game. She aimed her Folding-Compression-Tazer at the drone's starboard wing and fired. Seemingly all at once, the bolt from Kimber's gun scored a direct hit and the drone released another magnesium round, just as Jon finally made it to the dining room floor with a thud.

As the drone bounced off the walls, struggling unsuccessfully to right itself with only one engine, Kimber remained low to the ground and worked her way over to where Jon sat. She found him on the floor with his back to the wall, tightly holding a blood-soaked right shin. Kimber couldn't tell if the look on his face was one of pain, self-deprecation, or perhaps both.

She did a brief scan of the area and noted the remains of a wireless charging station. Since Jon's leg appeared to be intact, Kimber deduced that the projectile missed him and struck the charger, causing it to explode and peppering his leg and foot with shrapnel.

The still bouncing drone slammed hard into one of Navoa's stone sculptures and landed on the floor belly-up. Seconds later, a loud sizzling noise emanated from the device, signifying the frying of its own circuits to hide any electronic evidence it carried from its programmers or vendors.

Kimber sat on the floor next to Jon and smiled as she tapped the implant on the back of her left wrist three times, activating her secure mobile. "Control, this is Inspector Lee of the Governor's Bureau. I need a medic at my location A SAP; officer down, do you read?"

"Copy inspector, medical team en route; ETA five minutes. Any further traffic?"

"Affirm Control, tech team to follow from Central, if available."

"Understood GBI Lee; will contact with status."

Kimber let out an anxious sigh and took another look at Jon's leg. Without looking up at her he said "seemed like a good idea at the time." He shook his head and continued, "It's not as bad as it looks; just a flesh wound, or a dozen of them rather."

"The medics will be here in a few. Can you keep your foot from falling off until then?" Kimber responded with a concerned grin.

Jon gestured toward a napkin on the table and Kimber handed it to him. As he dressed his wounds he answered, "I think I'll make it, just don't talk my ear off in the meantime." Kimber couldn't help but laugh at the glib remark, which of course produced a weary chortle out of Jon.

His mirth made him wince in pain so he redirected his attention to delicately patting blood off his shin. Kimber grabbed a second and third napkin for Jon but her gaze kept resting on Navoa. Jon eventually joined her for a silent eulogy.

"Did we get this man killed Jon?" Kimber asked without looking away from the deceased man.

"Ouch. Difficult to say. He's clearly been under surveillance. Maybe his overseers didn't want to take any chances, even after all this time. The same thing could've happened with anyone. In any case, looks like we're making somebody nervous, which is a good day in my book."

SEVEN: CORRECTIVE MEASURES
TRUCKEE, REALIGNMENT REGION

Sidney Leyton ended what must have been at least his twentieth call of the morning. Each caller inquiring about one of two things: either the whereabouts of Dr. Shepard or the whereabouts of a data-module containing algorithms for the random-flux access codes of their client list. Without that module, their assessment teams would be unable to calculate what the codes would transfer to after their six-hour cycle, which would cause them to lose access to a large percentage of their continuous transactions and active clientele.

Sidney waved his hand over the infrared reader built into his desk, sending a message to his senior aide. A few seconds later, her image materialized on the opposite side of his hemi-hexagonal desk.

"Ms. Olin, could you alert the PR staff that I'll be transferring all my incoming, external calls to them for the time being? I have a few internal matters to attend to and they may take me a while."

"Certainly Dr. Leyton. Constable Fadil has also just arrived. Shall I send him in?"

"Ah, good. Saves me the trouble of calling for him. Yes, I will see him. Thank you Arasia," Sidney responded, pleasantly surprised. With another wave of his hand, this time with his palm down and fingers together, Sidney simultaneously closed the channel with his aide and cleared his desk of any open files being projected around the workspace.

Sabien el Fadil's sculpted form glided into the office as if he were wading through water. It always made Leyton wonder how such a fit person could move so elegantly. The constable halted in front of Sidney's desk like a Marine appearing before his commander.

"I take it your reporting in person without prompting isn't a good sign Fadil?"

"No sir, it is not. Two of my guardsmen are responsible for processing Dr. Shepard."

Leyton turned pale and his body went numb, which caused him to slump in his chair. "Processing? Are you saying they *killed* Miles?"

"That's correct sir," came his emotionless reply.

Now with his complexion rapidly shifting from pale to fury red, Sidney flew out of his seat toward his stoic chief of security, who still stood rigidly before his desk.

"What possible reason could your guardsmen have for killing the co-founder of this company!?"

Without blinking Fadil replied, "they were investigating the theft of classified company property and traced it to Dr. Shepard. The guardsmen promptly gave chase and he was eventually stunned by Agrarian perimeter drones after abandoning his conveyance."

Still on his feet, and trying to process what his security chief was telling him, Leyton wasn't quite sure what to say, but he knew the story wasn't adding up.

"Wait, you said they killed him. How could they do that in the presence of perimeter drones?"

"They were wearing class 4 electronic-dampening stealth suits, with multi-adaptive capabilities; which makes them invisible to most drones. They thought it best to contain the evident security breach rather than allow the algorithms to become exposed."

Leyton's shock could no longer keep him on his feet and he slumped in his chair like a corpse.

"Why would Miles steal technology he helped design, and what use would it be to anyone outside of the only system it has been keyed to?" he asked in a resigned lethargy.

For the first time since he'd known him, the constable's impenetrable façade showed a hint of uncertainty, which confirmed to Leyton that the situation really was as bad as it seemed.

"I don't have the answers to those questions yet sir, but the inquest is ongoing. The individuals responsible have submitted their incident reports and they are being cross-examined as we speak."

"Have you at least recovered the data-module?" Sidney probed poignantly.

Another crack in the armor. "No sir. The centurions of the Agrarian Region claimed Dr. Shepard had no such device on his person. His body and personal effects have been sent to San Francisco and are now under the jurisdiction of an inspector from the MUP."

"Oh brilliant!" Leyton roared springing back to his feet. "So not only is Miles dead, but he didn't even have what he was suspected of stealing, and apparently was not able to be immediately identified either. What do you suppose brought that about Fadil?"

Regaining his composure, Sabien straightened his dark-green uniform shirt and prepared his next answer carefully before he responded. "I am still examining the evidence on the theft, but it is my belief that the module was passed to a confidant. In regards to Dr. Shepard's lack of identification and readable features, it is my understanding that he has had extensive regenerative surgery, most of which was performed off the record."

"Last I checked, I still publicly run this company," Sidney began slowly. "Why am I just now hearing about all of this? I know Miles is a partner, and was not too happy about getting old, but that's no reason to keep me in the dark about prohibited activity, from *anyone*."

"Apologies sir, but, as a partner, I assumed you already knew of Dr. Shepard's abuse of resources, and why he continued to do so unabated. Aside from that, we only recently began to suspect him of corporate sabotage and didn't inform you because we had only suspicions."

"Then from this moment forward I want to be appraised of *all* security breaches, potential or otherwise. Understood?" Leyton asked loud enough for his aide in the next room to hear.

Fadil snapped back to attention and answered, "Understood sir! You will have my report within the hour, including my pending action requests." Following an approving nod from Sidney, he marched from the room without looking back.

~

After two unscheduled detours, Hal's hover-bus finally arrived at his destination; 40 minutes later than was anticipated. Although he couldn't be sure, a reverse image on another passenger's Google Glasses seemed to indicate that police activity on another route had caused multiple buses to compensate for the gridlock, but Hal had never been good at reading backwards.

Luckily for him he didn't have a schedule to keep. As Hal disembarked and the bus pulled away, he looked around the nearby building numbers to get his bearings. Hal had been to Fort Miley before, the most recent being just a couple of years ago; however it already appeared to have changed once again, as federally run campuses so often do.

Hal must've been standing there with a dumbfounded look on his face for longer than he realized because he didn't notice the repurposed golf cart pull up next to him. Behind the wheel was an elderly man wearing a wide-brimmed hat and vest covered in pins and patches of long-past conflicts.

"Can I help you young man? You look a little lost," the old veteran inquired in a slow, tired manner that conveyed his many years of experience and tragedy.

"I was just thinking," Hal began, "that it seems every time I come here something has been renovated and I need to learn my way around again. Is human resources still over there?" he asked pointing a bit to his left.

"Sure is, building 2, just on the other side of the canteen there. Hop in son, I'll give you a lift."

Hal sat down in the cart's deceptively comfortable passenger seat and it drifted away as smoothly as a boat on a lazy river. Clearly this guy's been here a while, he thought as they sped past the parking garage on his right.

"The SF VA Medical Center does have a way of confusing people, that's for sure" the older vet said. "Since it was founded in 1934, the place has expanded and contracted to meet the needs of both the VA and the city of San Francisco. Going to HR probably means you'll be talking to Mrs. Schell, that right?"

Startled out of his sightseeing by the question, Hal paused a moment, hoping he answered the question he thought he heard. "Oh, I don't know yet. I'm doing a walk-in hoping to get a lead on something, or at least add my name to a list of candidates who are immediately available."

The other man looked over and smiled in a way that suggested he knew something that would be awkward to divulge. "A walk-in huh? I can't remember the last time somebody's come here to do that. Maybe today's your lucky day though. Just lay it all out for whomever you talk to and I'm sure they'll do what they can to help you."

The cart pulled to an effortless stop and Hal became even more insecure than when he got in. He thanked the driver for the ride and advice, and started toward the building.

"You'll do fine son. Tell 'em Monte sent you; might be good for something." The vet chuckled and drove off at a snap.

After a brief walk and turn, just as Monte said, Hal found himself in a modestly furnished waiting room of two chairs, a generic piece of wall art, and reception desk on the opposite wall. There didn't appear to be anybody else around so he decided to take a seat and think about what he was going to say, if he even got the chance.

"Sir? May I help you?" came the alarmed greeting after what seemed like an impossibly short amount of time for someone to appear at the reception desk without notice.

"Um... Yes. I'm looking for information regarding any openings you, or the VA rather, may have for doctoral positions. I realize this isn't the way getting hired is normally done, but I'm new to the area and thought I'd take a chance by coming in personally."

Hal forced his mouth closed so he didn't continue digging a dubious hole for himself, and hoped the primly dressed twenty-something man behind the desk would at least humor him. That didn't seem too likely because the receptionist just stared at him as if he were frozen in place.

"If it helps," Hal continued, trying to break the awkwardness, "I was told to say that Monte sent me." As soon as it left his mouth, Hal knew he just made the situation worse.

The young man smiled and leaned back in his chair. "Oh, you know Monte? Ok, I'll see if Ms. Schell has a minute. Please have a seat sir."

Hal nervously did as he was asked but was stunned at how that chance encounter may have just saved his trip. He wasn't holding his breath though. A few minutes passed and a thin, blonde woman, who couldn't be more than a couple years older than the receptionist, appeared through a side door and gave Hal a mildly amused look before addressing him.

"Good morning. I'm the HR Managing Supervisor Monica Schell. I understand you're interested in learning what doctorate-level vacancies we have?"

Hal almost tripped as he stood up and hurriedly closed the distance between him and Mrs. Schell with his hand outstretched. He might have been able to hide his eagerness if he wasn't trying so hard not to appear desperate.

"Yes ma'am. Harold Dune, pleasure to meet you. Your colleague may have mentioned this already but I'm new to the area and am having trouble landing a job, what with the residency requirements of the region and all."

Monica let a reserved smile escape her aloof veneer, coupled with an understanding nod. "That can certainly put a damper on things if you're not prepared for it. Come on back, we'll see what we can do for you."

She led him through the door she appeared in and down a discreetly designed hallway with paintings of the SFVA in various eras lining the walls. There were only four doors along the hall, with an emergency exit at the end, and Mrs. Schell directed Hal to the second door on the left, after what appeared to be a very modern and sterile conference room.

Her office was densely decorated with personal effects: a few digital picture frames, keepsakes of all shapes and sizes from a healthy travel life, awards for children who had probably lost interest in earning them long ago, and several other items Hal couldn't identify. It was indeed a home away from home.

She gestured toward an antique-looking, but heavily cushioned, chair closest to the door. Hal assumed its position was so visitors could access the secondary interactive pad on the 'L' shaped desk and not become anxious about keeping eye-contact, which Mrs. Schell had so far been very good about.

"First things first, Mr. Dune, are you a veteran?" Monica asked getting down to business.

"Yes I am," Hal answered emphatically. "I was a Navy corpsman and participated in the campaign lovingly referred to as the 'Orient

Express to Hell' by the Marines I served with; of course officially titled Operation Errant Hunt."

Monica smiled and shook her head in a way that expressed a lack of surprise regarding the mindset of Marines. "Ok, that's a good start, but of course I'll have to verify that. Did you happen to bring a PDC?"

Hal dove into his pockets to locate his personal data card and was visibly relieved when he firmly grasped it. Not only because he remembered to update and bring it with him, but also because he was given the opportunity to use it.

He handed Ms. Schell the small, hexagonal device and she placed it on the embedded reader, which at first glance could be mistaken as a temperature-controlling coaster built into the desk. A faint, blue ring appeared around the chip as it loaded its data, authentication links and all. Then the ring's shade shifted to a light green when the download finished a few seconds later.

A holographic image of Hal's background information materialized at the corner of the 'L' at an angle both could easily read, validating Hal's assumption for his chair's conspicuous placement. As Monica skimmed the files, Hal developed an overwhelming urge to break the silence.

"I would've kept this data on my implanted PDC, but mine is the older model and not very sophisticated."

Without looking up Mrs. Schell replied, "I don't think I have the appropriate equipment to read those old ones anyway. Their encryptions were found to be insufficient by some standard that seems to change every month," she added matter-of-factly. "Everything seems to check out here. I'll run a cross-check of current vacancies, but as I'm sure you know our hiring process doesn't work... oh wow."

They both stared at a new display with the word PRIORITY in bold, red lettering floating about half a meter above the tabletop; Hal out of hopeful confusion and Monica from the amazement of not witnessing the alert before.

"Well Dr. Dune, it appears the gods are on your side today after all. Our parent company has an immediate plea for qualified doctors to fill regen-prep evaluator positions."

Hal wasn't sure what piece of information he should focus a reply on first. After a few breathless moments he decided on what confounded him the most; "I'm sorry, your parent company? Wouldn't that be the government?"

Mrs. Schell stopped what she was doing and slowly turned her head and body to fully face Hal. "Dr. Dune, the VA hasn't been owned by the federal government for several years. We're still managed by them... well, for the most part anyway, but for all intents and purposes we are one of the many arms of the Omnium Corporation."

Hal sat back in his chair deep in thought. "Omnium, the pharmaceutical and tissue research conglomerate?" He lingered an instant more to consider this revelation and shook it off. "Eh, no matter I suppose. What happens next?"

Monica eased out of her appraisal of Harold Dune and returned to her imager. "Well, Omnium's local office isn't far, just over in the Presidio. I could request a transport if you'd like, assuming you're interested in the position that is?"

"I'm not exactly sure what the job entails, but beggars can't be choosers I guess. Yes, I am interested and would be grateful for a ride if that's the next step. I have to admit though, I'm still confused by this whole turn of events. Is any of this even remotely normal in acquiring work at the VA?"

"As am I doctor, and no this isn't routine by any means. Certainly a first for me," Monica answered equally perplexed. She closed Hal's file and returned his PDC. "Your transport should be here in about ten minutes. They'll pick you up near the bus stop. Thank you for your service."

"I couldn't possibly thank you enough Mrs. Schell." They both stood, shook hands, and Hal found his own way out.

He stepped outside and had to shield his eyes from the sun as it began to peek out from behind a thick cloud, but he adjusted quickly and scanned the bus stop and landing pads looking for Monte.

He spotted one of the VA carts near the parking garage and picked up his pace, waving it down when the driver glanced in his direction. The cart veered toward him and Hal soon noticed that the driver wasn't Monte, but another aging vet in a similar hat and vest.

"Need a lift soldier?" the driver asked with a deep, southern accent when the cart pulled alongside.

Hal ignored the incorrect branch assumption. "No, thank you. I was looking for Monte actually."

"Monte's on his break, but I can give him a message if you'd like."

"Oh, sure. Tell him thank you, and that his name really does open doors around here."

The other man cocked his head back and laughed, a deep, single syllable guffaw. "Will do sailor. He'll appreciate that I'm sure."

Hal blinked at him wondering why the change in service and how he landed on sailor, when he was distracted by a bulky yet sleek transport landing at a nearby pad. He turned back to the driver and saw that he was already turning the corner at a distant building. He started toward the landing area again and quickened his pace; soon wishing he hadn't turned down the ride.

There was a garish icon emblazoned on the side of the vehicle that resembled an 'O,' so Hal presumed it was the one he needed. He smiled to himself when he considered how it would be just his luck to get on the wrong transport with his boost of good fortune for the first time in almost a month.

EIGHT: SURFACE TENSIONS

Kimber tuned out the report being recapped to her by the forensic technician, who was prattling on about his inability to retrieve any useful data on the drone, and watched as the medic attached the blue proderm to Jon's shin and foot.

She sat at the small dining table wondering if the skin-like sheet, designed to protect and advance the healing process, came in different colors, and who decided on blue in the first place? The tech began to walk away but Kimber stopped him. "Wait, are there any serial numbers or identifying marks on the drone that might be helpful?"

Technician Nerys spun on the ball of his foot to face Kimber, once more in palpable annoyance, both for his failure to look for such indicators and because he wrongly assumed she wasn't even paying attention to him.

"That's a good question inspector; I'll check and report back if I find something," he said somewhat snidely.

Kimber gave the tech a curious glance, noticing the attitude, and then turned back to see the medic helping Jon stand up off the floor. She leapt up to lend a hand.

"I'm alright," Jon groaned as Kimber reached out to steady him. "Thanks to this gentleman here, I'm in practically no pain. I was probably just sitting too long and needed to move around some. I've been told all the shrapnel has been removed," he concluded, giving the medic a hopeful look. The medic smiled and shrugged his shoulders while he packed up his equipment.

Kimber looked tentatively around the room to avoid staring at Jon's banded leg. She figured the evasion was too obvious so she decided to get back to work.

"I think we're about done here, without getting any further than when we arrived. Is there anywhere I can take you?"

Jon leaned against the wall at the end of the hallway and was delicately lowering his pant leg over the blue skin; trying not to get his now tattered, grey microfiber pants stuck on the rubbery material.

"Well, my lieutenant has already heard about my leg from the medic's incident advisory, so the most I can do the rest of the day is get my things from the office and go home."

He stood back up a bit too quickly and had to steady himself on the wall once again. "Whatever he gave me is pretty potent stuff," he said after righting himself confidently. "If you don't mind taking me back to the academy I'll check to see if my sensor bots turned up anything and just access the remainder remotely from my flat."

They left the now destroyed flat of the late Aramis Navoa, occupied by more people than had probably been there in the last seven years combined, and made it to the lift. Jon hobbled through the lobby and out to the cruiser with such a maudlin look on his face Kimber felt the need to reassure him.

"It didn't look that bad Jon. I'm sure you'll be fine in a couple days."

He slowly eased himself into the passenger seat before responding; "Oh it's not that. I'm just kinda pissed I didn't wear the pair of spider-silk defender pants up next in my outfit rotation. They probably would've stopped all those shards easily. But these are new and I wanted to break them in. Just my luck."

Kimber couldn't help but smile at his misfortune. "Can we say they're broken in now?" Jon just glowered at her.

~

The inspector dropped Jon off at his office and decided to go to the local Board of Inspectors Office at the former US Mint building off Market Street in the Lower Haight area. Since the use of physical money was a thing of the past, mints and some banks were now museums or historical landmarks. The Mint in San Francisco leased office space to government employees, which she shared with the Regional Parks Service.

She had a couple video messages from Dr. Mutara waiting in her official mailbox, but they were fairly lengthy so she elected to wait and view them at her office.

There was a tour going on as Kimber made her way across the tourist area of the mint. Apparently it was just beginning because she recognized the information being presented by the virtual tour guide from her many trips to the building.

"The Coinage Act was established on April 2, 1792 and the first Mint building was constructed in the nation's capital, which at that time was Philadelphia; making the Mint also the first federal building in the United States..."

Kimber tried to walk more softly on the marble floor but it didn't help to reduce the noisy clomps of her footfalls. She reached a non-descript door in a quiet corner of the large room, briefly looked to her left toward the camouflaged facial-recognition camera, and waived her right hand. The camera also checked fingerprints and read the embedded chip in her forearm, for access into the shared office areas.

Aside from the occasional escape route map, and display showing the status of the surveillance system, there were no windows or decorations of any kind in the hallway connecting the offices, and the lighting was government standard; dim and partially functional.

The individual offices were marked improvements over the drab passageway, but the Park Service's side of their mutual space was something to behold. There were plants everywhere, particularly by the window, and sometimes if the room was closed for extended periods of time, the oxygen buildup felt like a burst of adrenalin when the door was opened. Unfortunately, that wasn't the case this time, due to the door being cracked open, but it was still refreshing and remarkably relaxing for an office that was barely visited throughout the week.

The veritable arboretum was mostly made up of large, green-leaf plants, a few vines, and some flowers on the desk. Kimber spent several minutes watering them for her absent officemate before turning her attention to her bare desk and rickety chair.

Kimber sat down in her chair with a sigh, and balanced herself in the center so the chair didn't tip over. It had only been a bit over four hours since picking up the case and she considered passing it off to someone at homicide once Dr. Shepard's identity was confirmed, if it ever actually is she thought ruefully.

Remembering the messages from Erwin, she waved her computer awake and located her secure video mail log. Right away she spotted two additional messages waiting to be viewed; one from Jon and another from her boss; Regional Lieutenant-Governor Slade Wilkins. Due to the new messages being only a few seconds long, and the hierarchy of her position, she selected her boss's first, but also wondered why Jon didn't just call.

The imposing figure of the RLG filled the area above her desk and in his deep, baritone voice politely asked her to update him on the current inquest. Demandingly succinct as usual, Kimber mused, but a trait she appreciated most of the time to keep their interaction to a minimum.

Moving on to Jon's message, Kimber was taken aback by the cryptic nature of it; so much so that she watched it twice more: "Hi inspector... Um, my sensors got a hit on you-know-who's articles, but I'd rather not discuss them here. Gimmie a call when you get the chance, as well as the doc, ASAP. Thanks."

Great, she thought. The conspiracy continues. Kimber gestured to view Dr. Mutara's first message and made herself as comfortable as possible, because she knew it would take a while.

"Good day inspector. I've just completed my examination and while there's very little new information, what we did glean is quite interesting. Well, I think so anyway." Erwin took off an autopsy garment, in a very methodical manner, and eventually continued his message.

"Doctor Shepard's primary care physician was kind enough to send us *some* identifying information, and with that we were able to obtain two more definitive confirmations, as trivial as facial recognition and heritable indicators may be. In order for an unequivocal identification they agreed to send a representative out; who should be here at any moment..."

This reveal caused Kimber to sit up uneasily, accompanied by a squeak from her chair, and she paused the message from Erwin mid-breath. She couldn't recall of a situation where someone was sent to the morgue, other than to collect remains, in *any* of the several dozen inquests she'd either led or in which she'd participated.

People are still asked to identify bodies on occasion, but with advancements in medicine and other technologies, that practice had become extremely rare. Plus, requested identifiers are contacted personally and not sent by a patient's doctor or the deceased employers. Considering someone may have been killed to protect release of information, Kimber suddenly grew very concerned for Erwin and refocused before resuming the message.

"The interesting part, inspector, is that we discovered a sub-dermal data module that is virtually undetectable by most standard equipment, due to its location and composition. Although this is my official introduction to such technology, I've of course read about them via medical journals. They're generally implanted in the hip-area, or where the hands naturally rest for quick uploads, and are made out of a chimeric-like material, for lack of a better term, which not only evades scans but also mimics tissue."

Doctor Mutara held up a thin, oval-shaped object and turned it over delicately in his fingers as he looked on, quite impressed by the device. He placed it in a shirt pocket, probably so it didn't distract him any further, Kimber assumed, and looked back up into the camera.

"We found it largely by chance and, as far as I can tell, its memory appears to be full, or very nearly anyway. The data is encrypted and coded to a specific network, which I presume to be with his company. At this point I think it's safe to..."

The doctor was interrupted by a chime from another part of the room and Kimber could see his diener walk to the door on the side opposite his workstation. Two men in dark suits entered, showed their credentials, and in very short order were able to bring out a side of Erwin she'd only heard about in rumors.

Muffled voices couldn't hide the man's rage, but Kimber had no clue what it was about. For the next ten minutes, Erwin seemed to get progressively angrier, and then the recording stopped when he returned to his desk to open a line to the chief of police.

Before watching the second VM Kimber searched for clear images of the two men. Locating what she thought were the best, she enhanced them for even higher quality, then sent them through her face recognition software, as well as to Jon's mailbox. The next message opened with an exasperated Dr. Mutara.

"Try as I might, it seems the contractors of the Xedrix Consortium have more influence than the law itself. They came to the morgue under the guise of medical professionals but ended up taking the body, as well as our data, with them. I contacted three people, including the Regional Governor, and none of them were willing to raise a hand against the Consortium."

The doctor mussed his thinning hair with both hands in a detached manner, then, like a light switch, his face brightened into a devious smile and his next words came with more purpose.

"Little did they know we keep a remote backup of all data in the system for ten years, so all is not lost. Also, after they left, I remembered I still had the sub-dermal module in my pocket and I would be happy to deliver it to you at your convenience. There's nothing more I can do with it anyway. Message me when you can inspector."

Erwin and his lab disappeared and all that remained was a banner with the results of Kimber's image search, indicating that the two thugs did indeed work for Xedrix, but no full names, titles, or any other information was given.

Kimber sat a moment in thought, formulating how to arrange potentially two clandestine meetings in short order. She removed her office tablet from its docking station and leaned back as far as her chair would allow, though it was hardly any more comfortable than before. She began a query of Xedrix Consortium offices and found that their headquarters was in San Francisco, on the north east side of the Presidio. Realizing it was nearly lunchtime, she decided to invite Jon and Erwin to rendezvous for a bite to eat at a restaurant she occasionally patronized at the former Army base when Robyn left her alone on business trips.

~

Hal sat forlorn in the mid-sized transport and wondered why Omnium sent such a large craft for one person, and why a medical conglomerate needed such a vehicle in the first place?

The craft gently touched down on a landing pad surrounded by stretches of lush, grassy fields. Hal imagined the area would be crowded with tourists and employees of nearby businesses enjoying their break outside on nicer days, but the locals' standard of what constitutes as nice must be too high for that. There was still plenty of time for the weather to turn around to make that a reality after the work day however.

The dark green expanses were book ended by the all-too-familiar design of military craftsmanship nearly two centuries old. The vehicles had been routinely restored to appear as they did when the Army oversaw the entire Presidio, as well as several other forts and bases in the area until 1994.

A visual and audio announcement was made asking him to remain seated while the transport prepared for "terre-novo." A few seconds later, all the empty seats shifted to parallel the wall and Hal's seat smoothly advanced to the front of the vehicle. Once he was moved as far forward as was possible, the seat stopped. Hidden compartments opened and walls began to close behind him. The sequence completed and the front section of the transport separated from the remaining bulk, and quickly moved toward a large, modern-looking building to the north.

He passed Industrial Light and Magic, various shops, and multiple buildings of unknown utility before reaching a gate with the Omnium logo looming conspicuously overhead; it was a large 'O' with the rest of the name spelled out by an old EKG-style animated font. Hal noticed that it wasn't exactly the same logo that adorned the hull of the transport, and set a reminder on his watch to compare them later.

The vehicle came to a stop and the rear, left side melted away as naturally as it formed, revealing a grim–faced security officer standing attentively in a spacious but sterile light-grey parking bay.

"Good morning sir. Could you step this way for intake please?" the uniformed man asked in complete monotone. Hal did as asked and a scanning arm extended from the floor. A short tune played after a few seconds of it waving over him, the scanner disappeared back into the floor, and a door disguised as part of the wall opened nearby.

The guard brusquely thanked him and directed Hal to the newly-revealed entrance. As he boarded what appeared to be a lift, Hal glanced back at the guard and saw that he had different patches on each sleeve of his forest-green uniform. There was the same 'O' as on the transport on the right, signifying Omnium, and what appeared to be an 'X' on the left side. The door closed and Hal couldn't help thinking about ending correspondences as a kid with those letters, signifying hugs and kisses. The memory made him smile, and made the guard seem less imposing.

It didn't feel like the lift moved at all, but seconds later the opposite wall from where he entered opened with a mild hissing sound and Hal found himself in a large, open room with floor-to-ceiling windows that looked out upon the Presidio.

Aside from a few modern amenities, Hal felt like he went back in time to the 19th century. There was elegantly crafted wood everywhere: walls, floors, ceiling, and furniture. The many book shelves were filled with mostly leather-bound, vintage books, and there was even a wide-hearth fireplace, complete with natural-gas-created flames.

Hal's slow scan of the room ended when he noticed three people standing in the far-right corner, amongst a circle of antique fauteuil chairs, waiting patiently for him to acknowledge them. He walked over to the very fit middle-aged woman in the middle flanked by two younger men in nearly identical silver suits.

"Good afternoon Dr. Dune," the woman began. "I'm Administrator Kestra Katarn and these are my department managers Jacen Holt and Tristan Downing. Thank you for coming on such short notice." They all shook hands and took a seat, with Hal taking the remaining vacant armchair.

"Thank you for the opportunity to meet with you," he replied, trying to come up with something witty but not quite getting there. "I must apologize for my attire. I wasn't expecting my visit to Fort Miley to get me anywhere that would make it an issue; not this soon anyway."

Kestra smiled in understanding. "Well, when there's a pressing necessity for people with your skills we had to re-evaluate the process some. I'll assume I don't have to tell you about regenix, but what you may not know is that the demand far outweighs the supply. We've been reviewing the information you presented to the VA via your PDC. Is there anything not detailed there you'd like us to be aware of doctor?"

Hal's mind raced, trying to remember everything on his bio. He was confident his credentials were in good order. He was sure they knew he was new to the region, but perhaps they didn't know why he came here.

"I moved up here recently because there are more, better-paying prospects in my field than the region I came from. My wife wasn't quite ready to leave so we're temporarily separated until she is, or I move back down south, I suppose. The sooner I get settled, the sooner my son can visit, and potentially speed up the rest of that process."

The two men looked approvingly at Ms. Katarn and she nodded in agreement. "That sounds like great motivation doctor. We'd like to help you with that goal by offering you a probationary position of Regenerative Preparation Evaluator. The probationary period typically lasts six months to a year, depending on several factors, and you can start as early as tomorrow morning. How does that sound to you?"

Hal stared askance at the trio in a stunned silence. He couldn't believe that a couple of hours ago he was on a bus to the VA expecting to simply put his name on a lengthy list of potential call-backs when a vacancy opened sometime in the unforeseen future. Now he was being offered what sounded like an interesting job without even knowing what he'll be doing or where he'll be doing it.

"That sounds too good to be true, if I'm being honest. I'm afraid I don't know what that position entails or where I would be working if I were to accept."

"We can forward the position details to you for your review, but I'm sure a gentleman of your experience will have little difficulty grasping the duties," Kestra amiably replied. "The position requires a fair amount of outreach but you will primarily be working out of our main laboratory complex in the Realignment Region. A transport can collect you from your flat in the morning if that was your concern with the location."

Hal took a deep breath before answering, to try to appear at least somewhat professional instead of exposing the torrent of elation he actually felt. He finally calmed just enough to involuntarily stand and graciously accept their offer, causing the trio to follow suit and stand simultaneously.

"Excellent Dr. Dune, and welcome aboard. We will upload everything you'll need for both the position and tomorrow's orientation. Thank you for assisting us in our time of need."

Hal boarded the hidden lift in a giddy trance. When he reached the parking bay he told the hug-and-kiss guard that he could walk from there, since he lived only a few blocks away, and the guard pointed him to another concealed doorway that led him to the front of the building.

When he was a short distance away, he turned to regard the ostentatious office building. He could now see that Omnium shared its space with the Xedrix Consortium, whomever they were, and concluded that that was what the 'X' stood for on the guard's uniform patch.

The weather was gradually improving for the early mid-spring afternoon, or maybe it was just Hal's disposition. He noticed the Presidio Social Club from Lombard Street and recognized an Asian woman talking to two men, but couldn't place where he'd seen her before. He reached his block and was still thinking about the regally-dressed woman when it hit him; she was the one who almost ran him over earlier in the day! Huh, small world, he reflected, as the gate to his building magically opened a moment later.

By the time he reached the door to his flat his mobile alerted him that he had a new message, from the Omnium Corporation, and figured it was the job information packet Administrator Katarn promised. His mobile also reminded him to research the disparate Omnium logos, and Hal relished having afternoon plans that didn't involve traipsing around the city to follow up job openings.

NINE: LOOSE ENDS

Kimber had Jon and Erwin meet her at the Presidio Social Club on the east side of the historic area at one. Each person brought something to discuss, and Kimber hoped her suspicions about each of those topics were wrong.

She arrived a bit early so she could stake out the area; having her vehicle's computer randomly ID passers-by. Jon limped off a bus at five 'til and Erwin arrived promptly at noon. They picked a table outside the Club, under a covered awning, and impulsively skimmed the lunch menu that glowed from the table's smooth surface screen.

"No reason we should go hungry while we're here," Jon offered as he selected a few items. The others agreed and followed suit.

While they waited for their lunch Kimber wanted to get things started, but was distracted trying to remember the last time she shared a meal with anyone socially and couldn't recall when that was. She convinced herself this was technically a work lunch, and that concept seemed to help, but Dr. Mutara beat her to it by placing a glass evidence tube on the table. It appeared to contain a device made of skin-like material. He leaned in suspiciously, darting eyes and all, prompting the other two to do the same.

"Here's the data module from, I can confidently say, Dr. Shepard's hip. I haven't been able to retrieve any information whatsoever from it, except that it is nearly at capacity." He leaned back visibly relieved to have said his piece. Everyone looked at each other and the tube for several seconds before Kimber picked it up to take a closer look. She inhaled to speak but noticed a server approaching with their drinks, followed too soon after for a conversation, with lunch.

Kimber and Jon each ordered a sandwich: spiced soy patty on sourdough with Mediterranean lentil soup, and turkey club panini on rye with pomme frites, respectively. The doctor, on the other hand, had a dinner-sized plate of savory lamb chops and polenta. Erwin dove into his meal with the ferocity of a lion, while the other two stared at him in shock. He looked up at them sheepishly but didn't slow his pace.

"I rarely get red meat anymore. My wife will probably kill me when she finds out," was his explanation between bites, after he'd already devoured half his lamb. Kimber smiled and shook her head at this motley crew of covert agents.

Jon finished first, despite starting well after Erwin, and began his excited part of the mystery. "I have to get this out before I forget something. The dragnet of sensor bots I activated before going to Pacific Heights had a couple hits from the same source; they're passive programs so it's unlikely they were discovered. Also, Technician Nerys sent me the results of his inquest on the drone," Jon unconsciously rubbed his injured shin at the mention of that last word.

"Why he didn't send the report to you as well is anyone's guess inspector," he rejoined sardonically. Kimber just rolled her eyes and shrugged.

"Anyway, he says that the partial serial number recovered indicated that it was assembled in Cupertino. No surprise there, but there was a partial yet definitive 'X' logo laser-etched on the chamber for the magnetic-accelerator. So between the guys who strong-armed the doc, the sensor bots, and the bird of prey drone, all signs are pointing toward the Xedrix Consortium."

Doctor Mutara nodded thoughtfully as he scooped up the remaining bite of polenta. Kimber asked the question that had been nagging at her since she left the Mint; "But why them? Doesn't Omnium have their own internal security? I don't see the connection between the two."

Jon coughed, trying to answer too soon after taking a drink of his beer, but quickly recovered. "I wondered the same thing, so I did some digging. Apparently, while Omnium *does* have its own internal security at their main labs in Realign, they contract Xedrix practically everywhere else in their 'global operations network.'"

"So Xedrix may not even be able to read this data module?" Kimber asked, gazing through the tube that held it.

Their server came by and cleaned their table, which brought the doctor out of his thoughtful silence. "That's a good point inspector. They may keep their systems almost entirely separate. Luckily I think Omnium has an office nearby as well."

"They're in the same building actually," Jon chimed in. "Across the street from where Crissy Field used to be."

"A coincidence I'm sure," Erwin said cheekily, "but how does that help us? You're not just going to *give* them the module are you? Otherwise I'll just take it back right now."

"Don't worry doctor," Kimber reassured. "I have no intention of giving it to them; at least not until I find out what's on it. There must be a place at Omnium that can decrypt this thing; I just have to find a way to do that without tipping them off. Which leads me to what I have on the situation..."

She looked around, suddenly uncomfortable about the conversation. "Let's settle up first and relocate." Jon and Kimber split the bill to spare Erwin from his wife's wrath for a little while longer, and left the eating area of the Social Club.

They went to an open area near the parking pads and huddled together. "Ok," Kimber resumed. "I had a message at the office from Lieutenant Regional Governor Wilkins that simply asked for an update on the case. Then I watched your VMs doctor, where you mentioned that you also talked to him. I later noticed that your message came before his so I didn't want to give too much away when I called him on my way over here."

Kimber took a deep breath and was stretching some tension out of her neck when she noticed a man walking by who looked very familiar. He appeared to be curious about her as well, because he was staring in her direction. She couldn't place where she knew him from so she forced herself to refocus.

"Anyway, I gave him a basic rundown of the case. I didn't lie but I didn't tell him everything either. He asked what was holding up a confirmed identity and I redirected him to you, Erwin. I gather he didn't call you back?" Kimber asked with a grin that immediately incensed the doctor.

"He wouldn't dare call me back after our previous chat," Erwin replied in a huff.

"It was around this time he claimed to receive a press release saying Omnium had listed Dr. Shepard as missing and that he may have been kidnapped with property vital to the company's sustainment in his possession. I don't know if there's truth to any of this but that scenario could potentially fit this situation."

"Or it could be a smokescreen to save face," Jon cut in. "The kidnapping would fit if we didn't also know about the media white-washing and cover up with Navoa; assuming they're connected that is."

"Right. And my informant who put me onto him got back to me via secure text while I was on with Wilkins, with a list of agencies who have access to equipment that use bio-fletches. Omnium was on there, Xedrix was not, and I'm confident the list is accurate as well as current."

"What are you proposing inspector? Bluff your way into Omnium with that data module and hope they don't discover you before it's decrypted?" Erwin asked, voicing his and Jon's suspicions.

"Not exactly doctor," Kimber assured. "Governor Wilkins was kind enough to arrange an appointment with them. It just won't be for the reason I requested," she finished with a knowing wink and smile.

~

The trio hashed out a plan and parted ways; agreeing to at least chat about what transpired by the evening. As Kimber approached Omnium's main entrance, she reflected on that discussion with skepticism.

In her experience, the simpler the plan the less likely to make a mistake, but fewer mistakes doesn't necessarily equal success. Kimber forced back those insecurities and activated Omnium's intercom at exactly 1:00, when her appointment was set by the Lieutenant Governor.

"Good afternoon Inspector Lee," said a voice that was projected seemingly from nowhere, "do the results of our security scan meet with your approval?"

A mirrored window became opaque and listed all of her equipment: non-lethal FCT-II, variable secure mobile device (imbedded), personal identification chip-advanced (PIC-A), hybrid-composed data module... End.

Seeing the module on the list eroded her resolve some, but she answered in the affirmative. The door became a tinted-transparent window and opened with the sucking sound of an air lock. She stepped into a warm, well-lit waiting room with a slim black man in a tailored, silver suit waiting with his hands behind his back.

"Hello Inspector Lee. I am Departmental Manager Tristan Holt. If you'll follow me to the lift I will take you to meet with Administrator Katarn." He gestured to the hallway to his left and began rigidly walking down the dark corridor that became brighter the farther they progressed.

Mr. Holt didn't say another word the rest of the way and remained on the lift when Kimber exited into a room that was like walking inside a prism. Kimber couldn't tell where the windows ended and the mirrors began but judging by that, and the woman meditating on the floor in a business suit, she couldn't imagine a more suitable relaxation room.

Kimber began to slowly traverse the room when the sprawled woman stretched and stood in a remarkably elegant manner considering her business attire.

"Good afternoon inspector. I'm Administrator Kestra Katarn. What can we do for you today?" Refreshingly polite and to the point. A good start, Kimber thought.

"I've begun an inquest into identifying a body found just over the border of the Agrarian Region and the evidence strongly points to Dr. Miles Shepard; which Governor Wilkins may have already mentioned when he arranged this meeting," Kimber added, noticing Kestra looking somewhat bored.

"Actually, the Lieutenant Regional Governor provided very little detail into his request, but did mention Dr. Shepard," the administrator revealed. "If what you say is true, that is terrible news. How can I help?"

"I'd like to start by ruling out where he isn't. Do you have access to his calendar?"

"Yes, or I can in almost any other room rather. Let's go to a more practical work environment, shall we?" They left the prism room and entered the now vacant lift, then traveled horizontally instead of vertically, and entered a room that looked very much like where police conduct interviews or interrogations, depending on the situation. They sat around a small, triangular table and Kestra began manipulating what appeared to be thin air, from Kimber's perspective.

"Ah ha, here it is. It seems Dr. Shepard hasn't been to any of his appointments today. I also see that he was declared missing approximately two hours ago. When did the drones report the body inspector?"

Kimber sat back in her molded, polymer chair and waited a moment before answering. "Approximately sunrise this morning, but you already knew that didn't you, administrator?"

"I don't know what you mean?" Kestra replied with a bit of feigned shock in her eyes.

"I never mentioned drones Ms. Katarn. What else did the Regional Governor not tell you?"

Kestra adopted a smug posture and chose her next words very carefully. "I'll tell you that once you hand over the data module containing industrial secrets you're carrying, inspector."

The state of shock Kimber was in couldn't be noticed outwardly, at least she hoped so, but she was at a complete loss as to how Kestra knew about the module and what to do next.

"Our system is able to read most storage devices," Ms. Katarn began matter-of-factly, "but it makes things easier when it's our own technology. So what do you say we..."

Kestra's confrontational request was cut short by a tazer bolt shot into her leg that rendered her temporarily catatonic.

Kimber moved quickly to gain access to the data module, while attempting to appear like she was trying to help the docile administrator. She moved Kestra away from the computer's accessibility area with a sigh; this wasn't going exactly according to plan. As the contents of the module began to appear in the holographic projector, Kimber detached the bolt and started a mental countdown from 25 seconds.

Kimber looked at the holographic display with despair. The module's contents seemed to be nothing more than algorithms for Omnium's security system, or something, and what she assumed was a client listing organized by donors and recipients.

The countdown passed 15 seconds and Kimber was ready to give up when she noticed an untitled, unsent VM among the files. Without hesitation she uploaded the file to her imbedded chip and frantically began to cover her tracks as best she could, but realized how futile it probably was on the ubiquitous system. She closed all the programs and turned to face Kestra.

"Are you alright administrator?" Kimber asked as Kestra became more lucid. "Sorry about that. I didn't like where the conversation was going I guess."

If Kestra was only partially coherent a few seconds ago, Kimber's last statement brought her entirely back to sobriety.

"You shot me with a paralytic tazer bolt! Just to gain access to that smuggled data chip? Where I come from we call that assault and theft!"

"Whoa, hold on a second here. You bring me to the equivalent of an interrogation room, demand evidence legally obtained from a murder investigation, and expect me to not defend my mandates as a peace officer of the Pacific Union?"

Kestra sat several seconds staring at Kimber before replying. "The problem with what you just said, inspector, is that you don't investigate murders. And even if you did, that doesn't justify shooting me, with *anything*," she concluded with a waning confidence that showed her incredulity.

"That's a misnomer actually. I investigate missing and unidentified persons, no matter if they are dead or alive, and everything that is deemed applicable to that process. Since we have yet to definitively ID the body your security company somehow acquired before we could do so, I am obligated to protect the available evidence, administrator."

"Well, we seemed to have reached an impasse," Ms. Katarn began, as she adjusted herself back into her chair. "Perhaps we can barter to overcome this unfortunate situation? Allow me to download what's on the module, I will return it, and all is forgiven, barring some unforeseen variable."

Kimber sat back in her chair in an intransigent manner to try and hide the fact that she had absolutely no leverage. She knew that they were not going to let her out of the building until they got their data no matter what she decided. She saw no other alternative but endeavored to keep up her pretense.

"If I agree, what assurances do I have all really *will* be forgiven?"

"Ha, ha! None inspector," Kestra said in a deviously jovial way. "Either way, you aren't leaving here before I have a look at that data. Since you've already seen for yourself that there isn't any useful information on it, what harm could it do to allow our system to download it so we can part amicably?"

Kimber paused a moment before placing the tube containing the excised module in Ms. Katarn's open palm. The indignant administrator placed the tube on the scanner and began to operate the holographic controls again. After about a minute of what looked like conducting a symphony from Kimber's point-of-view, Kestra stood and returned the tube.

"I'll show you out now inspector," she said moving toward the lift door. The trip back to the lobby was awkwardly quiet, but once the front door was in sight Kimber quickened her pace. Suddenly, she was grabbed by both of her arms. She could see hands around her biceps but they were holding so tightly she was sure they had to be mechanical.

She struggled to free herself from the two large Xedrix guards but couldn't budge from their iron grip. They effortlessly picked her up and turned her around to face Administrator Katarn once again. Kimber's heart was beating so fast that the guard on her left must've noticed; he lessened his hold some.

"I'm a woman of my word inspector, and I expect no less from someone in your position," Kestra stated with a glint of pleasure in her eyes. "Just like the rest of the data on the module, the file you extracted was not meant for you I suspect."

The left guard kept his hold on Kimber's bicep muscle but grabbed her hand and extended her arm toward the other guard, while he waived a device over the imbedded chip in her wrist. Once that was done, they released her and the circulation in her fingers came flooding back with the sensation of pins and needles stabbing at her nerve endings.

"That file is now corrupted beyond repair. Thank you for your cooperation, inspector." Ms. Katarn pivoted on one foot and entered another hidden lift in the lobby.

Kimber rubbed her arms, knowing they'd be bruised tomorrow, and exchanged looks with the still silent guards when one of them gestured to the door. She walked slowly toward it, desperately hoping the auto-copy feature, which backs up anything saved on her chip to her secure mobile, was functioning properly and had gone unnoticed by their device.

Ten: Getting Acquainted

Hal laid back down after deactivating the projection of his clock, still set to military time. He had been tossing and turning since he went to bed hours ago, and checking the time every ten minutes wasn't helping. He called his wife and son to tell them the good news, and their excitement was infectious. But that wasn't the only reason sleep eluded him.

As fortunate and relieving as it was to be starting a new job in the morning, he couldn't shake the feeling that something was wrong with the whole situation. He felt confident there was a pretty high demand for qualified doctors, but going through the entire process in one morning still seemed unbelievably coincidental, and Hal didn't believe in coincidences.

Adding to that dilemma was the fact that he had only a vague idea of what his job would entail. Hal wasn't too worried about learning this new position quickly, but with all the controversy and expenditure surrounding regenerative surgery, combined with the day's events, he couldn't help but feel some ethical skepticism, if not outright suspicion.

Finally, Hal's eyes closed as he began his journey to unconsciousness, but in what seemed like seconds his alarm went off, letting him know that it was zero seven hundred hours. He was sure that it couldn't have been much later than two when he convinced himself to try and sleep, though he certainly didn't feel like he got any sleep at all.

A veteran's morning routine changes very little once one is established; sometimes even long after separation from service. No matter what the experience may have been, good or bad, structure and some semblance of control in life is difficult to go without for anybody who has had some, but particularly vets.

Despite running on less than normal sleep, Hal was still able to bathe, dress, and eat with more than a quarter hour to spare to wait for his transport at the designated area. As he lingered in the waxing sunlight, Hal decided to pace the sidewalk while continuing to research general regenix practices, and Omnium specifically.

There was quite a bit more history behind the theory-turned-science than Hal thought.

Regenerative science, in one form or another, has been a reality in the medical field for almost thirty years. It wasn't until the minds of geneticist Miles Shepard, biological engineer Sidney Leyton, and their respective research teams joined to create the Omnium Corporation that the practice became a juggernaut of medicine.

Hal stopped walking when he realized he had reached the end of the block, so he turned around to notice a craft on descent near his flat. He quickened his pace and met the transport as its doors opened.

The unmistakably utilitarian vessel was nearly identical to the one that took him to the Presidio the day before, albeit noticeably more worn. The most significant difference between the two was that there were other passengers onboard.

His addition evened the score of four men and women apiece; all appearing to be in their mid-to-late twenties or early thirties. As if it were choreographed, all briefly looked at him simultaneously then went back to whichever device held their attention prior to his arrival.

The transport lifted off as smoothly as a balloon being released and effortlessly headed east. Hal stared out the window in amazement at how fast they traveled, and judging by how quickly the landscape passed, guessed it was at least 800 kilometers per hour. He looked subtly around at his travel companions to see if any were interested in chatting but none looked up, or even stirred.

Lake Tahoe's perimeter started to break the horizon and Hal was shocked to find only 15 minutes had passed to cover the 200 miles from San Fran. A few minutes later the craft touched down at the manicured port of the Omnium Labs facility. The passengers all prepared to disembark and Hal started to think they all really *were* more machine than man. They all continued to move as mechanically as they had been since he boarded.

Once again the walls slid and folded to allow people to exit as if it were only an illusion. Everyone rushed off in single-file, leaving him alone to wonder if he was in the right place. After a moment of uncertainty his attention turned from the sprawling lawns and gardens to one of the women on the transport who had stopped and was now staring at him.

"This way please Dr. Dune. We unfortunately have a tight schedule this morning," the Indian woman, who was wearing athletic shoes with her navy blue business suit, told him impatiently. Hal reluctantly followed but quickly found himself struggling to keep up with her. Instead of lagging he decided to walk next to her in hopes of engaging in conversation.

"Thanks for showing me where to go. Hopefully I didn't make myself too obvious. I take it this isn't your regular detail, miss?"

She gave him a look that implied she was calculating the shortest response possible to avoid any further follow-up questions, but ultimately gave up, thinking it probably wouldn't work anyway.

"Patient Specialist Felinda Willrow. And no, I was asked to take you to the prep team because we were on the same transport. My regular duties are basically matching a part with a person," she finally replied without slowing her pace.

Hal considered his next words carefully, because his curiosity just wouldn't let Felinda's dubious hostility go as quietly as she might like.

"Sounds like a tough job. Must be satisfying when you think about all the people you help, but at the same time exhausting with the endless list of patients who will probably never know your name."

With that PS Willrow stopped in her tracks and stared at Hal, her mouth agape. After subjecting him to her piercing, quizzical stare for a few seconds she asked, "I wasn't aware the prep team needed a psychologist?"

"I don't know which is more telling; me getting you to stop, or your recognizing motivational interviewing techniques; or my poor excuse of it rather," he responded with a wry smile.

Felinda let slip an embarrassed grin, despite looking to the ground trying to hide it. "Well, I'd say you've missed your calling if I had any idea what kind of doctor you are. In any case, you're exactly right about my job, but it also doesn't help when our system is down, like it was yesterday, putting the entire corporation behind schedule. You'll probably hear plenty about that later, so shall we get on?"

Hal gestured his arm in the direction they were previously headed, "Yes ma'am, and thank you again for your help." With a nod and a pivot from Felinda they continued down the maze of intersecting walkways through the meticulously tended gardens of the landing port.

After traversing the complex a few minutes more, they entered one of the several identical red-brick buildings, all of which were so well maintained they looked as if they were just built. The only differentiation Hal could identify was that each structure had a Greek letter in more than once place by the doors. This particular one was a lambda.

The interior was equally disorienting, and it soon became obvious why those unfamiliar with the campus needed an escort. The floors were spotless faux-wood tiles and the walls were sky-blue fading into a white ceiling, giving the sense that one was in a tropical resort. There was no signage of any kind anywhere, so it was very easy to get lost and it discouraged people from wandering around to areas he or she shouldn't be in.

The only thing that distinguished one hallway from the next were color-coded lines running down the center of each wall, but still blending into the surrounding color scheme. They all appeared to be primary colors, at least in that building. Each side was different, with lines occasionally turning a corner and going down another hallway, or ceasing at a doorway.

Eventually, Felinda slowed when the blue line became dashed. She stopped to face a blue door, waited a moment for a biometric scan, then entered after it slid aside, allowing them access. What lay beyond was nothing less than a scientist's greatest fantasy, in any practically field.

Gleaming, state-of-the-art equipment as far as the eye could see. The mesmerizing hum of medical testing filled the air, and distracted Hal so much that he didn't notice Felinda approach one of the men in a white lab coat, who was hard at work. The pair exchanged pleasantries and walked toward Hal. The intense-looking man appeared to be in his late forties and gave Hal the impression of being of Japanese heritage.

"Doctor Harold Dune, I present Professor Tiberius Secura, but don't let the title fool you, he has multiple doctorates," Felinda chided sternly.

"I wouldn't dream of it. A pleasure Professor," Hal said extending his hand. Secura ignored the awaiting hand, and gave the rest of Dr. Dune a derisive look before turning back to Felinda.

"Thank you Specialist Willrow," the professor began in a deep, slow tone with a slight Polynesian accent. "We will take over from here. The system has finally been restored."

Felinda gave a short nod to Secura and turned to Hal. "See you on the flight back, doctor. Good luck."

Hal pensively watched her depart the laboratory as her last two words hung in the air ominously. He then turned to face the other man to find him staring at him so intently it appeared as if he were trying to read Hal's mind.

The staring contest continued for several seconds until the professor blinked and began an unprompted tour of the facility in his slow, deliberate style of speech.

After ninety minutes of mind-numbing details about the laboratory, the pair ended the tour in a small conference room with Secura waiting for Hal to sit oppisite him at the ring-shaped table, facing him.

"Now that you've been shown the blue team's work areas I suppose it is prudent to tell you what you will be doing," Tiberius told Hal condescendingly. "Until someone new comes along to give you an unofficial promotion, your main function will be to confirm or record the condition of specific patients who carry desired organs; dead or alive."

Secura looked up at Hal to gauge his reaction, which he hoped was unreadable; inwardly he was feeling quite relieved that he was being offered field work, at least until he's replaced apparently. Still, he was lacking a considerable amount of information about the job.

"Sounds interesting, and quite essential as well. Is one state of being typically a more common source over the other?"

The professor regarded the question as inconsequential but viable enough to warrant at least a vague answer. "It varies but on average is about equal. When on assignment you will be working with a diagnostic technician, who will be responsible for the portable equipment, but will likely not know how to use it properly. You will be expected to be well-versed in those tools, their use, and to stay updated with their calibrations."

Hal was waiting for some catch that would make him rethink taking this position, but when none came his subconscious decided to assert itself; "I look forward to the challenge. When can I start?"

~

The answer to Hal's question didn't come right away, but it did resolve itself much sooner than he expected.

He was eating lunch alone in the cavernous cafeteria when a man about his age, perhaps a little older, sat down across from him with just an apple in his hand. Hal continued to eat his lunch somewhat awkwardly; the man simply watched him as the apple crunched under his massive bites.

"Not bad food for a place like this eh Dr. Dune?" the man with thinning brown hair asked, finally breaking the ice.

Without showing surprise that the guy knew his name, and barely looking up, Hal answered, "The food's pretty good, but I'm more impressed with how big this place is."

"It's actually not that big when you look at it from the outside. The colors and little mirrors strategically placed around the room make it look bigger than it really is."

After another pause by the stranger, who Hal noticed was wearing an Omnium utility shirt, he stood partway up and extended his hand for Hal to shake, which he did with gusto.

"The name's Drinian. I'll be your tech today. We'll head out whenever you're ready doctor."

"Head out where?" Hal asked confused.

"To go organ shopping at one of the company's wards. The professor is under the impression you're were eager to get out of here for some real work."

Hal glared at Drinian wide-eyed for a few seconds until he finally understood what the man was talking about. "Oh yes, of course! I'm pretty much done here, but I should probably tell you that I don't know my way around the equipment yet; this being my first day and all."

"Wow, Secura must not like you or something. First day? No worries, he probably told you that techs don't know how to use their own equipment, but we do. We're just not supposed to use them without a licensed medical practitioner present, for legal reasons," Drinian responded matter-of-factly as he rolled his eyes and waved his hand dismissively.

"Well, that's reassuring," Hal quipped, hoping it didn't sound as sarcastic to Drinian as it did him. After a moment to see if his response offended the man, he continued.

"So where is this ward we're going to?"

"It's close, just one of the many retirement centers in the network the company owns. Take us about ten or so minutes by transport, on my ship anyway."

Hal scooped up the last of his vegetable side with his fork and placed the tray on the wide indentation in the center of the table for it to be collected, and stood up, his chair gliding back with a swish.

"I'm ready, just lead the way mister...? I'm sorry I didn't catch your last name."

"Didn't tell you what it was I suppose," Drinian said as the two made their way out of the cafeteria. "It's Posey, but everyone calls me by my first name so it rarely comes up."

The technician led them down a few quiet hallways that seemed rarely used, like secret passages, and Hal found himself back at the landing port much sooner than he thought possible.

Drinian deftly maneuvered them through the maze of waiting ships and vacant landing pads until he veered toward a shimmering utility van. Its glossy, black finish and silvery Omnium logo catching the high spring sun at just the right angle made it seem like a wondrous mirage.

As the pair approached within about fifty meters, the engine of the van automatically started and the vehicle gently lifted off the pad. At about ten meters, the doors opened downward, creating a ramp to accommodate its passengers, and hissed closed behind them once they sat in their respective seats.

Yeah, I could get used to this, Hal thought as he made himself comfortable in the soft leather, still impressed with the conveyance.

Drinian gave a few verbal commands and the van lifted off like a breeze. Hal was busy enjoying the view when Drinian decided to give him the tour.

"Each tech is assigned their own vehicle. I'm a bit of a gear-head so I've done some personal modifications on this one, with approval of course, mostly. Aside from *maybe* one of the executives' vehicles you won't find a smoother ride in the whole company," Drinian said proudly.

"The setup in the back is pretty simple," he continued; "equipment port, storage starboard. I don't think we'll need the storage units on this trip, since it's just a consultation, but we can carry anything back there. It's all labeled and pretty self-explanatory."

Hal nodded thoughtfully, still preoccupied with the craft, and assuaged by the task he'd been assigned. The ground was a blur beneath them as the ship rocketed to the north west. Hal had flown over this region many times in military craft, but he couldn't guess where they might be going.

The scenery grew more detailed as Posey's utility van slowed. Hal attempted to locate familiar landmarks and then realized he could simply check the onboard navigation system. It told him they were approaching Redding. Another set of coordinates indicated

how far away they were from the Shasta
Retirement Center.

"You could've just asked me," Drinian
said, catching his passenger somewhat off guard.

"What can you tell me about this center?"
Hal asked, evading the comment.

"Nothing to tell really. Most RCs are
pretty much the same. The only major difference
with Shasta I can think of is that it usually has a
higher concentration of veterans."

"Is that rare? I would've thought veterans
would be fairly spread out amongst them all."

"Oh, the vets are all over to be sure, but
Shasta is often used for intake when there's a
large influx of certain populations; it's fairly
transitional."

"Ah, there's your significant difference I
suspect," Hal mused. Drinian nodded and began
the landing sequence.

They touched down in a small courtyard
in the southeast quadrant of the complex. The
building was designed to be a large square with
one other small courtyard, actually used for
recreation by all appearances, and two larger
areas for intake transports, Hal assumed.

Tenants could be seen passing by the
windows of the landing area, but once they got a
good look at the ship they hurried like startled

rabbits; those who still moved without assistance that is.

Hal passed very few ambulatory individuals in the drab-grey hallways, to his surprise. Most were only in their late-sixties or early seventies and still reasonably able-bodied.

The Population Control Act of 2031 may have been repealed seventeen years after it was enacted, but many of its questionable policies still remained in some areas. One such policy was that all transient, disabled, and persons of public charge over sixty-five years of age who could no longer care for themselves must register with the Caprica Corps.

Due to the cost of living in California, and the burden of aging, there was no shortage of registrants, willing or otherwise. There was the occasional rumor about the Corps rounding up the homeless and addicts, as well as the mentally ill, and taking them to a place like Shasta against their will, but those reports were never substantiated to Hal's knowledge. Who wouldn't want stability and treatment, he reflected, remembering the many conversations with his colleagues at NCIS.

He paced the lobby as Drinian talked to a few staff members, whom he must've known judging by their familiar mannerisms, and locked eyes with a disheveled man not much older than himself sitting in a trac-chair. Hal recognized the man immediately, but couldn't recall from where until he spoke.

"This is no place for swabbies," the disabled man said in a voice so raspy that it was barely audible above the din. The man smiled, showing off his still perfect teeth and Hal walked over to greet his former gunnery sergeant, Elad McCallister.

"There's always room for a medic Gunny," Hal chided the man as they shook hands. "I thought you got a replacement leg after Fuchou?"

The light in Mac's eyes dimmed a bit at the mention of his mostly missing left leg. He patted what was left of it with a bittersweet grin.

"I did get a replacement; lost that one too when we retook Shanghai. Had a helluva hover-chair for a while after that, but I had to sell it because I was low on funds. Had to keep up this sporting figure," Mac said showing more teeth. "What brings you to Shasta Doc?"

"I'm supposed to be doing some client checks or something with my partner over there," Hal replied as he craned his neck toward Drinian. An intense shadow contorted Mac's face into pure rage, and the look he gave Hal sent chills down his spine.

"I *knew* it," Mac growled. "You're with those organ reavers at Omnium. Well I'm not going to let my, or anyone else's guts here go so some rich pederast can extend his life a few more years and take more parts from true Americans."

Hal stared at the man in complete shock and confusion. "Gunny, I don't know what the hell you're talking…"

"Stow it squid," Mac fired back. He pulled a pen-like object out of a vest pocket and jammed it into the power supply of his trac-chair. Lights and alarms began to go off on the chair but they were hardly noticeable in the noisy lobby.

Hal realized that McCallister had set his chair's battery to overload, and he recalled that those old cold-fusion cell-packs built up to critical mass very quickly under the right circumstances. Time and shielding weren't an option anymore. The only alternative was to put as much distance as possible between the chair and him, and try to take as many people to cover with him as he could.

"Everybody, clear this room right now!" Hal yelled as he ran over to a bewildered Drinian, grabbed him and the young female staffer by the elbow, and yanked them into a series of offices adjacent to the lobby.

Drinian protested and the woman yelped in pain but Hal ignored them and shoved them behind a desk. They started to get angry so Hal began to explain, but he was interrupted by a thunderous explosion that knocked him, and the desk, on top of the other two.

Before he lost consciousness, Hal heard the muted screams of the woman despite her being mere centimeters away from his ear, and he felt the heavy foam from the fire suppression system drip onto his neck and exposed left arm.

As the world faded to black, he pictured Sean's smiling face; the euphoria brought on by that image soothed the throbbing in his head, and eased him into a peaceful slumber.

ELEVEN: AFTERMATH

Kimber spent the rest of the afternoon deflecting the regional governor from what went on at the Presidio hours earlier, and assuring Jon and Erwin that she was ok from the comfort of her condo in Fairfield.

She didn't want to give them many details just yet, namely because she didn't have much to offer. Also, the sooner she put the fact that she probably should've been arrested behind her, the sooner they could focus on what to do next.

The three-way conversation ended with the promise of reconnecting as soon as new information came to light, along with the usual well-wishes from Dr. Mutara. With that out of the way, she refocused her efforts on the reconstruction of the downloaded file from the data module, which was thankfully still in her agency archive.

After she entered the appropriate passcodes to retrieve her archived files, a first for Kimber in the many years she'd been on the job, she located the most recent entry and selected what appeared to be a VM. A very much alive Dr. Shepard materialized inside what appeared to be the cab of a lorry.

> Forgive my haste, and the forum in which I present this revelation, but my name is Miles Shepard, co-founder and CFO of the Omnium Corporation. I am ethically bound to report that in the course of saving lives, at some point within the last decade, my company has been corrupted by influential parties who wish to keep obsolete laws such as the Population Control Act the status quo at the expense of morality and due process.
> Whether it's naïve optimism or plausible deniability that caused me to overlook such atrocities is anyone's guess, but I now have evidence of Omnium's crimes in the form of documented cases of unwilling donors, as well as transcripts regarding the sale of classified material to malevolent factions.
> To impede the destruction or alteration of this evidence, I have absconded with the company's processing algorithms, but I am currently being pursued by internal security guardsmen for my efforts, so my time here is short. If the data module this message is recording on is found intact, please get it to either my colleague Sidney Leyton at Omnium, or, if his position on the matter is compromised, my former student and confidant Gilad…

The message ended abruptly with a violent shake and slow blackout, reminiscent of a concussive electromagnetic mine. Kimber noted the timestamp of the recording as just over twenty-four hours ago, at Dr. Shepard's estimated time of death.

The inspector sat in thought for several moments. Being granted an interview with Dr. Leyton probably wouldn't be difficult, she figured, since the two worked together for many years at the same location. Suddenly she gasped and sat up rigidly in her seat.

She realized that although she was successful in copying one of the files from the data module, Omnium had the same information she did, and much more. Before she called Jon and Erwin she knew she needed to find Gilad before someone from Omnium or Xendrix did.

Kimber traced Dr. Shepard's career to its beginning via a Google search, and learned that he was a student-turned-professor at Stanford University, so she focused her search there. The list of masters students and doctoral residents who had worked under Shepard was staggering, which caused Kimber to slump back into her chair in defeat.

She sat there, sprawled in deep thought for a minute before she wondered why she was doing this the hard way. She verbally directed her computer to locate any re-occurring names within the same search parameters. A couple seconds passed and the machine chimed, indicating a completed search.

Kimber looked to see two names hovering over what doubled as her coffee table: Tobin Xiong and Keyan Dannik, with the latter name displaying double the entries over the former. She prompted the search aide to retrieve biographical information on Mr. Dannik, and there it was.

As her computer compiled the data, and organized it based on the police software she was using, the first line provided his full name as Keyan Gilad Dannik.

Kimber sat back up again, and intently skimmed Dannik's bio. His current employer, a military contractor in the Disney Region, suspiciously omitted his title and personal contact information from a law-enforcement search engine. Only his work number was provided, and she realized the line was opened before she had any idea what to say.

A fortyish Caucasian male with deeply tanned skin and well-groomed auburn hair that seemed to defy gravity, filled the holo-projector. He wore glasses that had frames larger than the lenses appeared to be, and had a fine-tailored maroon suit. Kimber recognized an away message when she saw one, but Gilad apparently took his profession very seriously.

"Good day. You have reached the office of Dr. Keyan Dannik. I will be off these premises from Thursday April 12th until most likely the following work week, attending to matters of a personal nature.

"If you need to reach me and don't have my private contact information, I can be found solving the following riddle: The man who invented it doesn't want it. The man who bought it doesn't need it. The man who needs it doesn't know it. Thank you."

Oh great, Kimber thought, one of *those* guys. She slouched back down on her sofa and tried to figure out the riddle. After a couple minutes of getting nowhere, she stood up in a huff and stretched, hoping Jon or Erwin liked riddles.

Both men watched both clips in silence. When they were over, Jon was strangely quiet while Dr. Mutara was smiling reverently.

"Do you have something to add doc… Erwin?" Kimber asked.

"Hmm? Oh, no, it seems pretty clear how we should proceed from here. I'm just enjoying being part of the intrigue."

"I'm not sure I follow. How should we proceed?"

"Why, by meeting with those two gentlemen of course," Erwin replied with a confused look about him.

"Tracking down Dr. Leyton shouldn't be a problem. It's this Gilad person I'm concerned about. I'm no good with riddles."

"Oh I'm dreadfully sorry inspector," the doctor yielded sheepishly. "That's a very old riddle describing a burial casket, or coffin as some still refer. Our Mr. Dannik is most likely helping to prepare Dr. Shepard's funeral arrangements."

At that moment Jon became a fury of activity, and Kimber assumed his earlier restraint was due to the riddle as well. In what couldn't have been more than ten seconds Jon found what he was looking for.

"There's a wake scheduled for this Saturday at a public house in Los Altos. The person it's being held for isn't mentioned, but who's setting it up is listed as K.G. Dannik," Jon reported.

Before Kimber could ask how he found that so fast Erwin scoffed, "A pub? Those Stanford types don't think much of each other do they, though I can't say I'm surprised."

"Public houses aren't the same as pubs anymore doctor. They're more like private clubs now. The use of the full term is meant to be ironic," Kimber responded with a smile, feeling somewhat gratified after the riddle gaffe.

"I've requested more information about the wake," Jon cut in, "but it looks like Gilad is staying at a hotel in Palo Alto based on his credit info. I'm sending both addresses to your mobile, inspector."

"Alright Jon, how are you getting this without an inquest notice?" Kimber finally asked.

"What do you mean? Standard search software can find everything I've mentioned pretty easily," Jon answered defensively. "The hotel info was a little trickier but credit companies already disclose *where* people spend their money, which is why those marketing vultures can find you so effectively. Matching the where with the how much is when the law draws a line for some reason."

Kimber studied the images of the two men and tried to come up with a response that hid her shame for not knowing that, but decided moving on was the more prudent reaction.

"It seems like we have a plan then gentlemen. I'll try to contact Omnium directly and set up a meeting with Leyton. Before that though, I'll stop at the Dark-Knell Public House to see if I can't run into Gilad, or whatever he wants to call himself."

All three nodded in agreement, as well as to also continue the clandestine decorum until a solution presented itself.

~

Hal woke to the hum of robotic arms applying what he assumed was proderm to his left shoulder and neck. Darkness slowly transitioned to shades of grey, then color peeked through and Hal realized he was in the civilian equivalent of a triage medical extractor; usually referred to as 'Timmys' by the Marines, and probably all police and military outfits.

The slightest movement of any kind brought on shooting pains all over his body, with the worst of it in his head and neck as he appraised his small environment.

Although there were no windows, Hal could tell he was not airborne. He'd been in similar craft dozens of times throughout his life and the telltale hum of engines was absent.

A scan of the area to his left bore nothing useful. Painstakingly, Hal rotated his head to the right and squinted to focus, but his view was blocked. He closed his eyes and relaxed his breathing until the ache in his head subsided. He reopened his eyes to a familiar figure standing by his bedside.

Drinian was in a disheveled state but with a relieved look so genuine Hal could do nothing beyond summon a painful smile. Aside from a brace on his left wrist, Hal could discern no other injuries on the man. He tried to say something to the tech looming over him, but his mouth and throat were so dry it came out as a whisper.

"Need… morphine," Hal finally breathed loud enough to hear.

"Doctor, this man's in pain! Can we do something about that?" Drinian snapped at what appeared to be a blank wall.

The telehealth monitors came to life as a physician at the nearest hospital was notified of the request. The system allowed practitioners to review the status of multiple patients at the same time remotely to triage more quickly.

A young Asian woman, probably fresh out of medical school Drinian assumed, filled one of the screens, while patient chart data and recommended treatments scrolled down the others.

"Amongst other things, he's being treated for a concussion," the doctor's soft voice explained, "but it doesn't appear to be too severe. I'm approving the request for a low-dose of morphine, and prescribing him a trauma relief regimen to tide him over the next few days. I'll approve a discharge within the hour, barring any unforeseen complications."

The woman vanished and one of the mechanical arms that had been applying the proderm injected something directly into Hal's vein. Almost immediately he began to relax as the pain melted away. A minute or so passed and he reached for the electrolyte-induced protein drink, feeling like a new man.

"Thank you Drinian. I think that did the trick."

Drinian grinned and leaned against the bulkhead across from Hal. "It's you I should be thanking Doc. You saved my life. I don't take things like that lightly. I'll give you a lift home when you're ready, and from here on out if you need anything, I'll take care of it; barring any 'unforeseen complications' that is," he finished with a sneer.

The room started to spin, so instead of trying to think of a witty rejoinder Hal lay back down and went over what happened in his stymied thought process.

A lot has changed since my corpsmen days, Hal reflected as he sat comfortably in the passenger seat of Drinian's modified utility van. The deft pilot took a coastal route back to San Francisco but said very little most of the trip. Hal recalled the sequence of events, but there were still a few questions he hadn't yet figured out.

"Why wasn't I interviewed before we left? I hope that was considered a major incident and not business as usual. No one seemed interested in taking my statement."

Without looking in Hal's direction, Drinian shrugged and responded, "First explosion I've had the pleasure of experiencing. I made a report while you were out. You'll probably be asked to give yours when you're feeling up to returning to work."

"But won't the police need that information sooner? Something like this would probably not escape their notice."

"It may have come across someone's desk, but Shasta is Omnium property. All of the retirement centers are actually. They'll either use internal security or their contractors to investigate most likely."

Hal thought back to the hug-and-kiss officer at the Presidio office. Seemed like a lifetime ago, but it was only the day before. A few minutes passed before he remembered the other part that was bothering him.

"The man who caused the explosion, I knew him. Served under him in the war. When he realized we were with Omnium he accused me of coming there to steal his organs. Why would he think that?"

The question got Drinian's attention and he snapped his head to regard the man in his passenger seat. After a few seconds he went back to piloting and twice appeared to try and answer but remained silent. Eventually, he sat back in his seat with a sigh and resolute look that implied a hard truth.

"Ok, I'm gonna level with you," he began. "You didn't hear this from me but this isn't the first time some, let's say, questionable ethics have come up with the company. Techs usually socialize amongst each other, but one was friendly with a few of the ladies in patient services. I believe you met someone who works there this morning.

"Anyway, he noticed consistent discrepancies between donors and product he collected and started asking questions. Word has it that the day after he brought it up to Secura, a few guardsmen paid him a visit and no one saw or heard from him again."

Hal mulled the story as the San Francisco skyline began materializing through the windshield. He recalled the friendliness between Felinda and Secura that didn't seem to be shared with anyone else; as far as he knew on his first day that is. His head still spun at every course correction, either due to the trauma or treatment for it, or both, but something about what Drinian had said sounded very familiar.

"How long ago was this? Hasn't anyone tried looking for him? I doubt your average corporate security can make someone just disappear. We're not talking about the mafia here."

Drinian glanced over apprehensively; weighing his trust in someone he just met a few hours before. Then remembered the life-debt promised at the Timmy.

"Happened about six or seven years ago. I'm sure those close to him put in some effort but we all contributed what we could when we could, including yours truly. It was different times back then; before the military contracts and absorption of competing companies within the state. Shouldn't be too hard for a smart guy like yourself to put some of those pieces together though, if you're so inclined."

Drinian landed directly in front of Hal's building, and even helped him to his flat. As he drifted off to a medication-induced slumber he wondered two things: how Drinian knew where he lived and what dosage of morphine that resident gave him.

TWELVE: CONSPIRACY

Doing his best to try and ignore the pounding in his head after only a few hours of recovery, Hal was reliving his NCIS days as he waded through files and articles related to regenix between six and seven years ago.

Ever since the communication industry consolidated under the remaining software companies, after those who had Chinese and Russian government associations were purged, altering web content became common practice, depending on who was looking to make such changes.

Those doing research or investigative work had to adapt in various ways, and with the right equipment Hal could compete with the best. He didn't have the right accesses at the moment, but he was still able to achieve some measure of success.

Hal came across several articles that were edited so haphazardly that he wondered why they weren't deleted altogether. In any case, the allegations against a VA employee, and his less-than-expertly rushed or covered-up legal proceedings, gave Hal the cues he sought.

Homeless Outreach Specialist Aramis Navoa was charged with multiple counts of kidnapping, fraud, and conspiracy to commit manslaughter. Thanks to an *incredible* plea agreement, those charges were either dropped or reduced due to mitigating circumstances.

Hal reread the most recent article on Navoa, dated yesterday, three times, and wondered if his alleged freak accidental death by an exploding charging station was what held Hal up on the bus to the Fort Miley VA around the same time.

There was nothing about a missing Omnium employee that he could find, but there was a very persistent advertisement linked to every article related to Navoa. Hal dismissed it at first, but its frequency became persistently suspicious.

The article was about the Farlander Foundation; a non-profit organization that raised money for regenerative surgery malpractice victims. The brief write-up was not helpful so Hal searched for the organization and found the connection.

Navoa was listed as one of the foundation's board members, alongside several names Hal didn't recognize. The story behind whom the foundation was named after, however, is what Hal found far more intriguing.

The pounding in his head subsided somewhat as he intently read the bio on Elim Farlander. Few specifics were given, but Elim was a modest yet respected member of the regenix community who disappeared attempting to blow the whistle on his company for potential ethics violations.

Hal read the whole history of the foundation but suspected crucial information had been omitted. He selected the 'contact us' link and was prompted to elect either donating or general inquiry. There were several ways to donate, but he was hesitant about opting for the inquiry, in case it posted on a public message board.

Having only worked one day in a month Hal wasn't in a position to make a donation of any denomination, so he prepared a message that had to be both vague but poignant enough to get a response.

"I'm interested in donating but I work in the business and am concerned about discretion on how the charges are listed. One of the many points that drew me to your NPO was the name. I used to know someone named Farlander. Could it potentially be the same person or a simple coincidence?"

Hal read through the message a couple of times before posting it. He then promptly made his way to the bedroom and collapsed on the bed as a combination of dizziness and the effects of medication overtook him.

~

After getting nowhere constructive in trying to locate her target at the public house in Los Altos the next morning, Kimber decided to stake out the hotel in Palo Alto where Gilad was assumed to be staying.

Sitting in the lobby of the Four Seasons, Kimber wondered what tangent Jon might be prattling on about at that moment. She then considered, possibly for the first time, that maybe she missed the big lug for how effortlessly he could cut through the tedium. However, as quickly as it occurred to her she dismissed it as simple boredom, preferring active police work rather than the idleness of stake outs.

She was about to order her third tea of the morning when a man dressed like a rock star strode by the lobby café at a brisk pace. He was barely average height, but his three-piece metallic blue, pinstripe suit and designer, wing-tip shoes would probably cost her a month's pay.

The man was nearly to the front doors by the time Kimber realized he was the man she sought. She leapt up and ran to intercept him before he reached the exit.

"Dr. Dannik!" she yelled while still only halfway across the reception area. He stopped dead in his tracks, as if he were frozen in time. Then, as Kimber arrived close enough to slow her pace, he cautiously raised an arm to clear his MX mirrored Google Glasses. He didn't turn around so she walked the extra few steps to face him directly.

"Dr. Dannik? My name is Inspector Kimber Lee of the MUP. Do you have a moment to answer a few questions about your former colleague Dr. Miles Shepard?"

Gilad appeared visibly relieved but didn't budge from his stance. "You say you're from the MUP, yet you wish to discuss someone who is clearly found and identified," he responded in the same soprano monotone from his video message.

Kimber showed him her credentials and that was enough to convince him to at least move toward the café area. They went back to her table where the third cup of tea awaited her. She offered Gilad a cup but he declined.

"I am part of a small team who was responsible for identifying Dr. Shepard, before Omnium took his body that is. We recovered an imbedded data module that contained a video where he denounced Omnium for ethics violations and mentioned you by your middle name. I could only guess he did that for at least *some* measure of anonymity, but would you mind elaborating on that doctor?"

Gilad became more uneasy the longer she talked, so Kimber decided to allow him to control the direction of the conversation and let her question linger.

"Does Omnium have this video as well?" he asked after a moment of contemplation. His posterity was obviously the priority before revealing anything hazardous to his health.

"They do, but it took some digging on our part to find you, so while they'll likely track you down eventually, feel confident knowing your middle name has remained relatively incognito, for what it's worth."

"It's only a matter of time," he said in a disassociated state while staring at Kimber's steaming tea. "Even sooner if they ask Leyton about it, but it's doubtful they will."

"Why do you say that, and who's 'they'?"

"Omnium's internal security. It's headed by a man named Sabien el Fadil, who was essentially forced upon Sid and Miles to take over security when Omnium signed with the Department of Defense, through ambiguous intermediaries, to be their sole regenix supplier. Miles saw through that poor excuse for a contract immediately, but Sid is the trusting type."

"Dr. Shepard mentioned having evidence of Omnium's crimes. Would you know anything about that, or Dr. Leyton's potential involvement for that matter?"

Gilad gave her a peculiar look that she would describe as sizing her up. The level of trust that she asked of him to have in her couldn't be gained over a ten-minute conversation. But he realized that he may now be in danger no matter what he tells her. It's either vindication or vengeance at this point in his mind; his personal adaptation to fight or flight.

"I am almost certain that Sid will know nothing about Omnium's perfidy, being the veritable patsy that he is. However, since that is also how most who know him would describe the man, he makes for the perfect mark to hide damning evidence. I don't know exactly what you should be looking for, but it may be somewhere on or near him. Now if you'll excuse me, I have a wake to facilitate."

Kimber waved her hand over the table's card reader to pay her tab and hurried to stride alongside Gilad.

"You seem quite convinced of Leyton's lack of complicity. He is the CEO after all."

"Inspector Lee, you referred to Miles as my 'former colleague' but we were never that. He was my mentor for a time and then we became... friends."

Gilad paused thoughtfully as the hotel's auto-valet sprang into action. He finger-combed his hair to calm his nerves and continued with the look of a man contending with his conscience.

"Omnium wasn't always the façade of success it is today, so to help Miles out, I pulled a few strings with DOD contractors. I'd worked with government freelancers of different sorts for years by that point so it was a simple task. The contract was ludicrous, turning the founders of

Omnium into little more than figureheads, amongst other things of equal uselessness.

"Sid didn't see it that way and pushed the deal through. Miles always had qualms about the situation, and today you tell me he was killed talking about evidence against Omnium."

A company car with a logo Kimber didn't recognize silently drifted up. Gilad sat at the driver's seat but paused before closing the gull-wing door.

"Between the incredible guilt I'm feeling for putting Miles in that position in the first place, and my wish to see justice served with the same mercy he received, there is an unwavering notion that the answers you seek will be with Sidney Leyton somewhere, whether he's aware of them or not."

She inhaled to form a response, but Gilad closed his car door and sped away without even looking in her direction.

THIRTEEN: APPREHENSION
SACRAMENTO, CAPITAL REGION

Kimber wasn't quite ready to head to Omnium Labs in Truckee. She needed to avoid reassignment, and figured making an appearance at the main office could buy her a few more days to work on the Shepard case before she was ordered to close it.

After her crash seven years ago, she preferred to use her cruiser's flight capability sparingly. Since time was not on her side at the moment however, she decided to make an exception. To minimize risk of collision and hard landing, she opted to navigate the San Francisco and San Pablo Bays, then turn up the Sacramento River toward the capital.

The trip through the waterways was like stepping back in time. Ruins of ages-past industries. Generations-old housing communities. Empty lots where someone's livelihood once stood.

Kimber was surprised that more of the waterfront areas weren't renovated or claimed for one of the many tech companies to come and go over the years. Nevertheless, she always noticed something new or different each time she went this route.

The skyscrapers of the capital began to appear on the horizon and Kimber requested her onboard AI to connect to her building's parking area controller and prepare for landing. Almost immediately the cruiser decelerated and positioned itself to land in the riverside employee structure, near the pyramidal Ziggurat building.

Home to the California Department of General Services since its construction in 1997, the ten-story ancient Mesopotamian-inspired structure also houses several other departments and agencies, both state and federal, whose funding didn't permit them their own building, such as the MUP.

Kimber made her way to her seventh-floor office, and received the same confused looks she always did, often by the same people, as if she were a new employee. Since she can do her job from practically anywhere in the state, as well as Hawaii and parts of Nevada, she went to the office as little as her boss would allow. The dubious stares amused her almost enough, however, to want to stop by more often. Considering the option, she smiled at the irony that doing so would negate that particular source of entertainment.

The proximity reader unlocked the unmarked employee door as she approached it. The public entrance was just around the corner, but Kimber hadn't seen it in so long she had forgotten what it looked like.

The dull, government standard accommodations were in full effect there, and probably the entire building. The beige walls, light-grey cubicles, and charcoal-colored carpet did little in the way of motivation. With the dozen or so staff always coming and going, few people were there long enough to make any changes that would improve the look and feel of the place.

Kimber's work space was closest to the door; best for unseen arrivals and departures. She listened for a few seconds to verify if anyone else were around, but it seemed more eerily quiet than usual. It was policy to have at least two inspectors in the office during regular working hours, so she knew *someone* was around; however, he or she didn't make their presence known.

She activated the desk's availability indicator, which signaled the office manager that she was there, and sat down in her still new-looking chair. Kimber was barely off her feet when her desk holo-projector lit up with the head and torso of Cindal Olin, the office manager; practically startling her back out of the seat.

"So you really are there! For a second I thought your desk was possessed or something. How you holding up inspector?" Cindal asked in her usual perky tone.

"As good as can be expected Cindy," Kimber answered with a sigh. "Where is everybody? It's a ghost town back here."

"Oh, Jace and Lorian are around here somewhere. Probably just stepped out for an early lunch or something. Wilkins is on the warpath though, for *you* apparently. He asked me to notify him if you came in, so I'd turn off your avail if he's not high on your contact list today."

Kimber smiled in respective awe. Cindal was always looking out for the inspectors; particularly her, and she never understood why she got such special treatment.

"Thanks for the warning but I'll give him a call. He's half the reason I came to the office anyway."

"And the other half?" Cindal asked with pseudo hopefulness in her voice.

"To see you of course!" With her day made by that comment Cindal switched off, but not before she rolled her eyes.

After the holo-projector went dark, Kimber prepared for her next conversation with some deep breathing and neck rotations to loosen up a bit. She hoped Cindy's use of the word 'warpath' was an exaggeration as the connection with Lieutenant Governor Slade Wilkins was going through. She doubted it though. He answered and was talking so fast that Kimber assumed the conversation had started before he picked up the line.

"If this is a bad time sir I can call back."

Wilkins was taken aback by the interruption but was quick to respond. "Not a chance Lee. We have a lot to talk about, starting with why you're pretending to be a homicide investigator on a case that's been closed by this office?"

Kimber chose her next words with care, but remained unwaveringly apologetic. "That body was never officially identified as Miles

Shepard sir, but since there's a high probability to that conclusion, I thought it wise to cover our asses on such a high-profile victim."

"So this *wisdom* of yours led you to think that attacking an executive at a multi-billion dollar company, one that the military and hundreds of police departments contract with by the way, to gain access to their intellectual property was a good idea?"

"Sir, as I explained this morning, I had evidence recovered from the morgue that I was bringing to Omnium for assistance with identifying the body. They refused to cooperate, accused me of stealing trade secrets, and Ms. Katarn was hit by a stun bolt during a scuffle with security."

Wilkins leaned back in his chair, crossed his arms and stared ominously at Kimber. To her that look meant one of two things: he knows she's full of crap, or he merely suspects it but doesn't have enough to call her on it.

"Yes inspector, I recall your statement on this matter. I also remember closing the case minutes after you gave that report. Why then are you still meeting with people connected with Dr. Shepard?"

"Trying to give the man's next of kin some closure, and following a lead that may explain the recent influx of missing persons," Kimber replied with complete sincerity, though surprised she revealed the concept with so little evidence.

The lieutenant governor appeared genuinely intrigued. He was very much a by-the-numbers bureaucrat, but a mystery still caught his attention from time to time. Plus, the man made a name for himself by never shying away from a good fight, no matter whose feathers were ruffled in the process.

"What does Shepard have to do with that unfortunate trend? Where are you getting this information?"

"Between what little info we could glean from Shepard's autopsy, an informant with DHS, and what I gathered from my trip to snob town, I have sound reason to believe that Omnium is deep in the throes of a cover-up. That is why I want to request authorization to question Doctor Sidney Leyton."

"After your performance at their Presidio office I doubt Dr. Leyton's security chief will allow you on any of Omnium's properties if he can help it. However, given the seriousness of these accusations, I'm going to grant your request on a provisional basis.

"You have 48 hours to skulk around and report back to me, *from your desk* preferably, and we'll go over what you've found, if anything. I'll contact Omnium and tell them to expect you, but if there's a repeat of yesterday's imprudence or you fail to convince me of your claims, that will be the end of it.

"Thank you for asking permission rather than forgiveness this time. Don't make me regret this latitude I'm giving you inspector. You also have other assignments pending so I suggest you work fast."

Kimber opened her mouth to express a rare level of gratitude, but Wilkins had switched off before she could. With the clock ticking she said her good-byes to Cyndal and left for her potential meeting with Omnium's CFO, Doctor Sidney Leyton.

~

Kimber was back in her cruiser heading east. Jon and Erwin were on her heads-up display and she caught them up to her current plans.

"And you're headed to Omnium now?" Jon asked.

"Over halfway there," Kimber responded. "I'm taking the scenic route though, so it's still about an hour away. Their internal security may not even let me talk to Leyton but Gilad was pretty sure Shepard left something behind for us to find and present to... someone."

"If true inspector," Erwin chimed in, "anything not already confiscated would likely be in plain sight, and therefore almost impossible to identify without the autonomy to search freely."

"That's part of the reason I'm taking the long way, so I can think of how to do that very thing doctor."

"Well Shepard and Leyton worked together for a long time," Jon continued. "Maybe there are some good memories to keep him focused on that will put you in his good graces; unlike apparently the other Omnium executive," he said giving Kimber a derisive smirk.

She responded with a mocking grin but liked the idea, and Erwin nodded thoughtfully as well. She had considered a similar tactic already, by using more guilt though, but Leyton wasn't what she worried about. Being allowed to see the man may be the hard part if Wilkins was unable to come through for her.

"The LRG was supposed to arrange for an appointment but I'd like to have a backup plan just in case. Jon, can you see what's available regarding their security; who, what, and where? Doctor, try to find a direct way to contact Leyton, via complaint or customer inquiry. I'll re-open this line in forty minutes and go with what we've got."

Everyone agreed and signed off. Kimber continued along Old Interstate 80; the new one was a couple kilometers up via the public transit lanes. Old 80 was hardly used anymore, due to the improved public transit system, so it had been reduced to probably a quarter the size it once was.

Kimber didn't really know why, since it was entirely the wrong area, but going this way always reminded her of the Donner Pass legend. The 86-party wagon train was held up for four months in the Sierras during a particularly harsh winter in late 1846 through early 1847.

Just over half of the party survived to tell the tale in the spring, and the manner in which they made it through had a few certain coincidental connections in Kimber's mind when considering Omnium's suspected illegal activities.

The time came to reconnect with Jon and Erwin so she re-opened the shared channel. Both gentlemen opened their respective channels immediately and relayed their news. Jon discovered nothing helpful regarding the company's internal security, but the doctor had more luck.

"I started with a provider inquiry regarding a mismatched product tag," Erwin began, "which is a genuine complaint in this case, and was transferred to a patient specialist named Felinda. After some brief chit-chat I revealed that my patient was Dr. Shepard, and that there were anomalies with his autopsy.

"The young lady took several seconds to respond but once she did I was put in contact with Dr. Leyton's administrator Arasia Somtay, where I promptly explained who I was and why I reached out to them. I informed her that a representative of my office was in route with sensitive information for Leyton specifically and gave her your name inspector."

Kimber's onboard pilot alerted her that the town of Truckee was approaching, but she paid the announcement little attention due to her impressed amazement at Erwin's improvised subterfuge.

"Are you serious doc? Just like that?" Jon asked breaking the stunned silence.

"Quite serious detective. You're to proceed to a service entrance at gate epsilon inspector."

"Wow doc... Erwin. I'm speechless. Well done. I still don't know if Wilkins followed through, so you may have single-handedly made this trip worthwhile. Remind me to never play cards against you." They all shared a subdued chortle and signed off, though Jon hung his head a bit before his image faded. She made a mental note to throw some praise his way next time they chatted.

Gate epsilon was like driving into a secret military bunker, like when she toured the Green Briar in West Virgina. The downhill grade went on what seemed like several minutes, with no other vehicle in sight. Kimber checked the clock as the anxiety began to mount, but only about ninety seconds had passed by the time she reached the bottom.

The space resembled the average parking garage except two notable differences: there were no other vehicles of any kind to be seen, and one wall next to where the gate guard she met before her descent indicated she park was completely covered by color-shifting LEDs that seemed to respond to movement.

The polished doors of a lift opened on the wall adjacent to the rainbow wall, and a tall, imposing man in a dark-green uniform stepped out.

"This way please, inspector," the guardsman said in a deep baritone.

Kimber nodded and made her way to the opening. "What's with all the lights? Looks like Times Square over there," she said as the doors to the lift closed in front of them.

"It started out as an experiment in mimic kinesics, but was moved down here as added security because people can't resist making the wall move; except you apparently," the guardsman sullenly retorted as he gave Kimber an annoyed look that implied he was done talking.

The doors opened to another man in a dark-green uniform standing as still as a statue with a long, brightly-lit hallway stretching out behind him. The Persian guardsman was smaller in stature, but his obvious military discipline more than made up for any physical shortcomings he may have compared to the first man, Kimber discerned.

He made a robotic, yet swift, ninety-degree left turn to face the elevator. I'll take it from here Olin," he said to the taller guardsman, but looked at Kimber.

The other man came to attention, acknowledging the order, and then took on a more resigned stance, but remained in the elevator.

"This way please, inspector," the smaller yet apparently higher-ranking man said as he spun on his heel and began to walk the opposite direction. Kimber practically had to jog to keep up with him.

"You guys run a tight ship here," Kimber breathed nervously as she came alongside the man. He didn't acknowledge her presence in the least but she knew he heard her.

"Thank you inspector," Fadil eventually answered in a mechanical tone, "but let's dispense with the pleasantries for the moment shall we? Since we have recovered our critical data from you I inferred that the danger you pose at this point is minimal. But that still begs the question of what you hope to accomplish from this meeting?"

Kimber was taken aback by his forwardness, but she did her best not to let it show through.

"I figured Dr. Leyton might want a few details on the death of a close colleague of many years; as well as tie up a few loose ends to wrap up my unidentified person case."

"Such as?" came the curt response.

Kimber delayed a few seconds while she decided on an answer that wouldn't get her black-listed from Omnium right then. She tried to make it appear that she was simply out of breath; a ruse that was not far from the truth.

"Primarily to see if Dr. Leyton knew what Dr. Shepard was doing the days and weeks leading up to his death, and specifically why he might have been trying to conceal his identity to such an incredible degree."

Suddenly, the security chief stopped in front of a large piece of digital wall art and looked at Kimber quizzically. He held out his hand in a snap-motion pointed at her.

"Questions I too would like to know the answer to. Surrender your tazer please." Kimber begrudgingly handed it to him. "It will be returned to you before you depart, depending on your manners. Good day inspector."

The art moved in a receding way to reveal a transparent door leading into a plush waiting room. The doors parted silently and Fadil lingered immobile as she entered.

Kimber felt some mild relief as she took in the principally Asian décor; possibly Tibetan she figured. Abstract renderings of ancient temples covered the walls, while sculptures and spirit houses occupied the horizontal surfaces.

After a few curious paces into the room she noticed an Asian woman emerge from behind a perfectly camouflaged desk. Kimber thought she looked to be from the same cultural region as most of the art in the room but wasn't sure, and she was older than her but only by a couple years.

"Hello inspector. My name is Arasia Somtay, Dr. Leyton's confidential secretary. He is prepared to see you now."

Kimber thanked her while admiring a particularly intricate spirit house. She turned around to see another hidden door open next to Arasia's desk, with the secretary directing her inside. She thanked the first polite person she had met at Omnium, took a deep breath, and proceeded into what felt like stepping a thousand years into the future.

FOURTEEN: KEEPSAKES

The office was a sterile, slate-grey, mausoleum of a room. Yet it was much more alive with digital activity compared to the serenity of the previous room. The walls were almost completely covered by monitors and projections, displaying a variety of goings-on throughout the world.

Kimber recognized a few media stations, as well as what appeared to be security feeds, but there were also displays of detailed transactions streaming by in which the commodities were tissue and medical supplies. A few more screens were stock tickers, both foreign and domestic, and one very prominent display near some shelves in the corner on her right looked to be showing a movie from the twentieth century.

She spotted Dr. Leyton standing behind a massive, polished dark marble desk, close to the same color as the flooring, with every millimeter of its table top covered in electronic devices.

"Don't get lost in the foray inspector," Sidney warned, "you get used to the sensory overload eventually."

"I don't plan to be here long enough for that doctor," Kimber countered. "Why bother getting used to all these distractions in the first place?"

Sidney smiled condescendingly, "I come here to work. All of this data is essential to do that work at some point, but thankfully not often all at once. How can I help you inspector?" he asked, as he gestured to one of the lounge chairs in front of the desk.

Kimber sat, not sure which surprised her more, the strangely awkward seat or her suspicion of Leyton having no idea why she was there. She did her best to get comfortable and decided on the most direct course of business.

"Dr. Leyton, has anyone told you why I asked to see you?"

"I was informed that you were with the MUP, so I assumed you were here about Miles. Thank you for recovering our algorithms by the way, if that was indeed you."

Kimber cringed inwardly at the mention of her visit to Omnium's Presidio office, but dodged the subject entirely.

"So you're aware of the circumstances surrounding his death, and subsequent evasive tactics your company representatives have placed into the path of this inquest then?"

Sidney frowned at the accusation, but not as an affront of denial; more of a sad acceptance.

"Since I see no reason to deceive you inspector, namely due to knowing your part in this matter has ended, I will tell you that Miles was accidentally killed while fleeing from a pair of our guardsmen because of purportedly pilfering those industrial secrets I just thanked you for recovering."

"His death was hardly accidental doctor. A banned biological weapon was what killed him, but stranger still was that virtually none of his internal organs were originally his."

That revelation clearly stunned him. He sat back rigidly in his much more comfortable-looking chair and sighed.

"I've only recently learned of Miles's misuse of company property, but I've been aware of his growing dissension toward a few of our contracts for some time; which has a certain irony about it when those two issues are put together I now notice.

"We've been friends for many years, but colleagues for even longer. We didn't agree on everything; a considerate conflict that only made us better business partners, for a time. I also trust my chief of security. When I learned about Miles's indiscretions, admittedly after his death, I was naturally shocked, but left the situation in his more objective hands."

"You still trust your chief constable despite me pointing out three discrepancies in his transparency in the few minutes we've been talking?"

Sidney transitioned from an offended expression to one of contemplation before he responded. "What was the third one?"

"Well, it's clear your chief didn't keep you informed about a close associate's activities, or the actual purpose of my coming here. Your guardsmen used illegal projectiles that you weren't aware of. And, even though you consider Dr. Shepard a friend, all of your recent knowledge of him seems to be coming from your security chief instead of from the man himself. Who's actually running this company Dr. Leyton?"

The question got his attention, but not in the way Kimber thought it would. Sidney's face contorted in grief, and he limply hunched further into his chair. He quickly composed himself but could no longer look Kimber in the eye.

"I should've listened to him before it was too late. To be perfectly honest with you inspector, I don't have an answer to your question. Miles was able to avoid the bureaucracy of it all somehow, but I've been little more than a figurehead for years. A well-paid figurehead I assure you. Not much beyond that though I ashamedly admit."

"For what it's worth doctor, Dr. Dannik assumed that very thing. He also thinks Dr. Shepard has more faith in you than you may realize; if that helps you sleep at night."

The mention of Gilad got Sidney to look Kimber's way again. "Keyan was always the pragmatist," he breathed, "but I don't know what you mean by the faith remark."

"Did Dr. Shepard give you anything recently he thought was important? A keepsake, a unique souvenir, a cherished piece of memorabilia?"

Leyton looked at her wide-eyed, as if he'd just been roused from a dream by some terrifying imagery. He stood and made his way to a display case sandwiched between two bookcases opposite the office windows, where the classic movie was playing.

"Miles was a collector of movie memorabilia. I don't know when he started his collection, or why really, but it's all either authentic or officially certified, and is worth well over a million dollars."

He reached up and carefully lifted a black, boxy item from one of the shelves and walked it back to his desk.

"This is an authenticated replica of Spock's tricorder from the original series of Star Trek of the 1960s. Leonard Nimoy was an idol for Miles. They even shared the same birthday.

"Even though he was still quite young, Miles sought out anything he could find related to Spock when Nimoy died in 2015, and this was his most prized possession from that collection. It seemed rather strange that he would entrust this to me, but even more so that you would ask about it a week after I received it."

"I'm afraid it gets stranger still doctor. For reasons I can't get into right now, I would like to borrow that item with the promise to return it as soon as possible."

The conflict going on inside Sidney's head was palpable. After a full minute of internal debate he stood up and delicately placed the tricorder in front of Kimber.

"I expect this to be treated with the utmost care and respect inspector. If this meant as much to him as he claimed, then the sentimental value of it to me is ten-fold."

"You have my word that it will be well taken care of doctor. Thank you for entrusting it to me," Kimber said as she stood and placed the shoulder strap of the tricorder around her.

They exchanged parting pleasantries and she set off for the exit. Kimber ventured about halfway out when she spun around to see Dr. Leyton still standing behind his desk unmoved.

"When I return this, would it be possible to arrange for a tour of this facility, in case I decide to make a radical change in my career path?" she asked with a sly smile.

"Certainly," Sidney responded somewhat aloof as he transitioned back into executive mode. "If I am able I will show you around myself inspector."

Kimber thanked him and gently patted the tricorder like she would to console a child. She waived to Arasia sitting quietly in the decorated foyer on her way back to the parking garage and wondered where she would retrieve her tazer.

~

Kimber returned to her cruiser without anyone saying a word to her. Aside from the awkwardness of the silent guardsman in the lift, she thought it suspicious that Security Chief Fadil didn't want a follow-up interview regarding her conversation with Leyton. When she reached the garage, the tall guardsman handed over her tazer and she departed as hastily as she could without drawing too much attention.

She was about twenty minutes out of Omnium's empty underground lot, and well into the darkening skies of evening, when she finally noticed there were two VMs awaiting her.

The first was from Jon, checking in to see how she was doing and to let her know that he'd be going back to work in the morning. The second was from Wilkins, who informed her that she had been assigned a missing person case out of Stockton. The uploaded case file appeared in a separate box precisely as Wilkins briefed the case, almost as if he timed it that way.

She was about to return Jon's call when her vehicle's proximity alarm sounded. She slowed a bit and checked her displays but saw nothing within the meter-wide range of the alarm's sensors, and no other hazards were evident.

The prox alarm is activated when traveling at speeds greater than 50kph. Kimber estimated seeing only about a dozen other vehicles on her return journey thus far, so she figured there was a malfunction in the system. She had verbally begun the order to run a sensor diagnostic when the words 'Unauthorized System Access' appeared on her HUD.

She scanned the exterior displays again and gasped when she noticed a strange shadow extending beyond her cruiser's shadow. The vertical viewport was activated, and through the light mist she recognized the Yeager-class scout craft as it lingered above her aft quarter.

The agile, one-person air ship was widely used in the war for its stealth and maneuverability, and its effectiveness was immediately apparent. In seconds her cruiser's systems began to fail, and Kimber realized that she needed to put more distance between her and the blade-shaped craft to break the link to her onboard computer.

She hit the accelerator and attempted a few evasive maneuvers, but the Yeager was still on her. Sweat began to bead on her forehead with the dread of knowing what she had to do to shake this hitchhiker rushed over her like an arctic wind. Flying low across the water at a leisurely pace was one thing, but dogfighting was something else entirely.

As the car's attitude began to fluctuate, Kimber punched in the code for an emergency takeoff with an extended booster. There was a five-second countdown as additional engines warmed up and other systems came alive with activity. Kimber inhaled when the 2 was announced, and a second later the cruiser shot into the air at a sixty-five degree angle, which buried her body into the car seat.

She steered the now airborne car toward the nearest sky lane, after it leveled off following completion of the booster cycle, but the Yeager rapidly gained on her.

Kimber ordered her computer to recalibrate its security protocols, in hopes of slowing a second system hack if the craft were to catch her again, which seemed inevitable.

She knew that most Yeagers were at least lightly armed, so she assumed the one chasing her was as well. Aside from a few tactical drones and SWAT vehicles, general police craft were prohibited from deploying lethal weaponry by law, but models used by Skyway Patrol and her cruiser came with a surprise or two that could turn the tide when appropriated.

The Yeager was nearly on her again. She would not be able to reach the sky lane before he was in range to hack her computer. Kimber's hands started to get clammy as she waited until her pursuer closed to three meters for maximum efficacy.

The distance melted away. The scout craft was now taking up her whole display. Finally, his range read three meters and she pitched nose down while hitting the brakes.

The Yeager raced past. As it did Kimber activated a short-range electromagnetic pulse, normally used to stop fleeing vehicles. The Yeager's impressive maneuvering allowed it to achieve a partial turn before its engines shut down.

Civilian cars and public transports were built with a safety feature to prevent collision with the ground or other objects after an engine failure; but safety wasn't as high a priority for military craft, for cost-cutting purposes. The Yeager spiraled toward the ground as quickly as it sliced through the air when giving her chase. If there was an ejection pod it either didn't work or the pilot was too proud to use it.

Kimber reported the crash to the local Skyway Patrol but didn't loiter to investigate. She had a pretty good idea of what she might discover about the pilot or the craft already, so she resumed her course back toward the Bay Area along Old Interstate 80, but adjusted her onboard AI's sensitivity to be more vigilant just in case. By the time she arrived at Jon's flat to get a head start on the tricorder, she was still reeling from the second time Omnium tried to kill her in as many days.

FIFTEEN: SERENDIPITY

The sound was as gentle as tapping a wine glass, but to Hal the computer chime was like a giant gong in his head.

He rubbed his eyes until he could focus on the time as it floated above his nightstand and saw that it was 4:03 a.m. He stared at the numbers in disbelief, and then realized he was on the brink of falling off the end of his disheveled bed and righted himself by flopping inward like a fish out of water.

When some of his grogginess subsided, he choked down another dose of medication prescribed by the triage doctor, and quickly drained the mildly chilly room-temperature glass of water from his nightstand.

He assumed the meds needed to be taken with food, as most that work well do, so he grabbed a protein enriched fruit-oat bar on his way to address the noise coming from his computer.

Hal wasn't sure if his holographic screen looked especially bright due to the darkened flat or his concussed state, but either way the new message icon felt like it was burning his retinas.

Thank you for your interest in supporting the Farlander Foundation. The brave individual this Foundation was named after was not a celebrity, so the probability of knowing him being a coincidence is minute.

Regarding how donations are listed; not to worry. It will appear as 'Exemptible non-profit' on your report. Feel free to follow our online prompts to make a donation at your leisure. If you are seeking more information than what general searches may provide, one of our advocates will contact you. We appreciate your inquiry and look forward to your generosity."

Hal read through the message once more, feeling clearer with each passing moment as the concussion meds took effect. He closed the display and drifted back to bed; this time under the covers. He set the alarm for 7:00 a.m. His eyelids became heavy in seconds. Despite his near unconsciousness, part of the message replayed in his mind like a looped audio file. How would they know when to contact me? he thought, before sleep overtook him.

~

The transport to Omnium Labs in the morning was more uncomfortable than the day before. Every time Hal looked away from the window into the cabin a handful of other passengers would awkwardly glance away.

At first he thought the stares were due to their surprise at his being back to work the day after surviving an explosion; a notion that amazed even him. Then, about halfway to Omnium, he discovered some of the proderm on his neck had been dislodged from frequent scratching and was poking out over his collar.

Hal did his best to tear off the dangling ends of the synthetic skin in the lavatory before he reported to Secura, though he doubted the man would even ask how he was doing, or care for that matter. Fortunately, he didn't get the chance to prove his pessimism.

As he approached his work area, a man in a green uniform blocked his path. Still somewhat dazed from events the day before, Hal nearly collided with him.

"Good morning Dr. Dune. I'm Chief of Security Sabien El Fadil. If you would please follow me; we need your statement for an incident report regarding yesterday's transgressions."

Without waiting for a response, Fadil spun on his left foot and began walking briskly down an adjacent hallway. Hal glanced between the blue-outlined door and the rapidly shrinking, green-garbed man a couple of times before he ran to catch up to him.

An interestingly wordless seven-minute walk later they arrived at the security hub of the facility, and Hal suspected much more went on there than simple security operations.

The room was alive with wall-to-wall monitors and projections, as well as the buzz of communications of every kind. Men and women floated around tending to the various automata like hummingbirds to flora.

Hal was led to an unimpressive interview room with only a table computer and two speciously uncomfortable chairs. He relayed his story as detailed as he recalled to prompts projected above the table and was released with a tepid 'thank you' by a mechanical voice.

On his way back through the gauntlet of tech, Hal couldn't help but notice that there was an obvious focus on an Asian woman with angularly-cut hair. He made it to the security room door when he realized that he'd seen the woman before, twice.

Hal stood staring at the dozen or more monitors that featured her as if he were scrutinizing a museum piece. He must've been stationary for some time because every guardsman in the room turned to look at him almost synchronously. One of them pointed to the door and Hal made the final three paces out to the hallway with giant, curved windows that looked out onto an eccentrically opulent courtyard.

Two questions echoed in his mind as he attempted to find his way back to the Lambda Sector: what was she doing here and why were so many resources dedicated to watching her? This was the third time their paths crossed in as many days, and Hal didn't believe in coincidences. Maybe she's here to investigate the explosion in Omnium's Shasta facility? he wondered.

Despite what Drinian had said about Omnium looking into their own, internal matters, his curiosity got the better of him and he altered his course toward the dining hall; where she appeared to be located a moment ago based on all the security monitors.

~

It was too early for lunch so there were very few people in the cafeteria. Hal had to think quickly because it looked like she was getting a tour and was nearly ready to move on.

He briskly walked to the nearest coffee station, filled a cup half-way with hi-caf, grabbed a fruity-oat bar, and chose a route that would intersect hers while pretending to absent-mindedly stir his beverage.

Even with the ruse he must have been quite obvious, because the astute woman gave him a few suspicious looks before he finally bumped into her, almost spilling the hot drink.

"Oh, I'm terribly sorry! The caffeine hasn't quite kicked in yet I suppose and... Say, you look familiar. Wait a minute; didn't you nearly run me down in your cruiser the other day because I was, well, not paying attention, like now?"

A look of recognition briefly crossed Kimber's face, but she tried to hide it since Leyton was staring right at her. She was about to play dumb when her escort cut her off to break the awkward staring contest that had followed.

"Come now Dr. Dune. I know you're still recovering from yesterday's events but I hope

I'm not witnessing some contrived courtship ploy that's far older than even I am."

The tall, slender man gave Hal a skeptical look as he waited for a response. Hal casually shifted his head from the piercing sneer offended by what he assumed was an executive of some sort to the woman, and hoped he wasn't too deep into a hole of professional humiliation.

"Strangely enough Dr. Leyton, what this man says is correct. I probably wouldn't have recognized, Dr. Dune is it, if he hadn't said anything. Hopefully our close call didn't contribute to whatever happened yesterday?"

As deftly as he could, Hal attempted to put, who he now understood to be Omnium's Chief Financial Officer, in a vulnerable position while simultaneously making the officer suspicious for more data.

"Difficult to say officer…?"

"Inspector, Kimber Lee."

"Oh, pardon me. I doubt it did Inspector Lee but I'm sure Dr. Leyton here can tell you all about the Shasta Center. It's only my second day and I still have a great deal to learn about the company. Speaking of which, I should get back to it so a third day can be in my future. Good day to both of you, and my apologies for the interruption."

Hal eventually found his way back to the blue team's office in Lambda Sector; still carrying a long-since emptied cup of coffee. He worked with another lab specialist to familiarize himself with the regenix process, Omnium's policies and procedures, and his specific role in the office.

It all seemed to be quite important information, especially considering Hal knew only pieces of it beforehand, but he was too busy going over the encounter with Inspector Lee in his mind to give the helpful specialist his undivided attention. The young man stopped more than once to ask "what's with the grin," but Hal played it off as being thankful for the assistance.

~

Leyton was impressed and relieved with how quickly Kimber returned the tricorder, so he kept his word of personally giving her a tour of the Omnium Labs. The place was indeed extraordinary, if not a bit too squeaky clean like most laboratories were, she suspected.

The people were even more peculiar. A unique work culture may be an explanation, but many of Omnium's employees behaved like drones or automatons. They had practically no personality that Kimber saw, save for Dr. Dune.

Kimber finished her tour without a second mention of the Shasta Center, but it remained foremost in her mind. Not only that, the run-in with Dr. Dune caused a perceptible shift in Sidney's decorum. He acted more uneasy and hurried the remainder of her tour, but the reduced small-talk was refreshing.

The tour was just a formality though; trivial to what their next move would be. When Kimber had Jon examine Shepard's Star Trek memorabilia, he discovered a code disguised inside the tricorder's refurbished data screen; once Jon was able to get over the awe of handling the device that is.

They debated their options after the mysterious code was recorded into a pair of data sticks. Erwin had also been consulted, but he came to the same conclusion they reached: an avenue must be found to upload the code onto Omnium's network, either via informant or personally.

Kimber sensed Doctor Mutara wanted to discuss additional alternatives, but his wife somehow learned he had eaten lamb for lunch the day before and was not about to let him off the hook to eat out again unsupervised anytime soon. Erwin signed off but was able to sneak a couple messages out that morning.

As soon as she departed Omnium's vacant, underground parking garage once again, and made sure she didn't have a tail for a second time, Kimber contacted Jon at the Academy to see what he could find about Dr. Dune. The more she learned about the man, the more confident she became about enlisting him into their group.

"I don't want to get my hopes up Jon, but his charming ruse of bumping into me at Omnium may be the luckiest break we've had in this entire case."

"So *that's* what's considered charming these days. Maybe it was delirium caused by the explosion at Shasta," Jon reproved mockingly. "Do you think we can trust him?"

"Everything we've found on him tells me we can. Let's pay him a visit to potentially prove me wrong."

"You, wrong? I wouldn't miss that for the world, inspector."

~

Hal spent the ride back to the city reflecting on the vast difference between his first two days at work. Being blown-up aside, spending some time outside the Labs compared to a full nine-hour workday at the office was a *much* better experience he thought.

He almost contacted Drinian to see if he could take him home again, but planned to do so in the morning instead, for a potential lift to work. Perhaps if I put myself out there early enough I could land another outing, he theorized.

The shuttle dropped him off at the usual spot, two blocks west of his flat. The sun had nearly set, so shadows from the buildings stretched like gigantic fingers across the street. There was little foot traffic about at this hour but Hal figured it was the lull between returning home from work and forming plans for the evening.

Since civilian cars were no longer allowed to park on the streets in most large metropolitan areas of California, the police cruiser that sat in front of his building was quite obtrusive. As he approached his security gate, he realized he recognized the vehicle.

The passenger-side window disappeared into the door and the same pair who pulled over in the rain two days ago regarded him once again. Inspector Lee cocked her head slightly to the right in an amused manner and then spoke.

"Good evening Doctor. This is Officer Jon Colquitt of the SFPD. I thought it best that our fourth encounter be on purpose this time. Might we come in for a chat? You can tell us more about Shasta which you so tactfully brought up earlier today."

Sixteen: Parsimony

"Sorry about the mess," Hal warned candidly. "I'm still moving in and I don't spend much time here."

"It's been a month doc," Jon reminded. "What are you waiting for?"

Hal gestured to his chaise and half-sofa, ignoring Jon's question. He went to his fridge to see what he had to offer his first guests to the flat.

"I wasn't expecting visitors so all I have to drink is water, beer, and cold-brew coffee."

The pair of officers looked at each other as they settled in opposing seats and simultaneously answered "beer."

Hal grabbed three Anchor Steam ambers and expertly opened them without a bottle opener, which prompted impressed stares from Kimber and Jon.

"I was a sailor. I know how to drink on a professional level," he said shamelessly. Amused grins replaced the stares and Hal sat on some boxes facing them in his quaint living room. They each took a swig and Kimber broke the silence that followed as the intoxicant percolated into their system.

"I understand you moved up here from the Disney Region, doctor. Your wife and son are still there for the time being?"

"That's right, but nobody there calls it that. It's either the Lucas or Marvel Region to the locals, depending on where you stand with which property contributed more to saving the company once the Anaheim Park and Burbank Studio went up in smoke."

The guests both nodded thoughtfully, but shared a dubious glance while their heads were still in motion. "So what's your take doc?" asked Jon.

"Lucas, no question. That company spread out its resources all over the Bay Area long ago, and was barely affected by the earthquakes and revolts within the industry in the south.

"Oh, and to answer your other question inspector, my wife and son will join me once I've settled in, and she's completed her commission with the Marines."

Kimber shrugged at the comment and redirected the conversation to cut through any further small talk. "If you don't mind doctor, please give us your side of what happened at the Shasta Center, since any other source we find likely won't provide the whole story."

"Certainly. But first, it's Hal. Doctor is just a title, inspector," he teasingly rebuked. Hal recounted everything he remembered about his first day of work in a detailed summary. Jon took a few notes on his folding tablet but Kimber listened intently, not looking away once while he talked.

"So this former acquaintance of yours," Jon interrupted, "accused you of collecting organs from nonconsenting donors, and blew up his chair to stop that from happening?"

"Well, 'former acquaintance' doesn't really do our service together justice, but pretty much yeah. I wouldn't say he was accusing me specifically *per se*, but he was definitely alleging this with Omnium. He called them 'organ reavers.'"

"Aren't you the least bit curious to find out if the gunnery sergeant's claims were true, so that his death wasn't in vain?" Kimber probed, hoping to strike a nerve.

"That's a little melodramatic for a guy who killed about a dozen innocent people and injured many more on an assumption. I'm not one to believe in coincidences though, so I've started some digging of my own. Haven't turned up much yet but each piece has a place in the puzzle." Hal paused, taking a sip of beer before continuing.

"I take it you need me to confirm or deny this information somehow at Omnium, since transparency isn't exactly a significant part of their business model?"

The two officers exchanged surprised looks, then Jon answered suspiciously, "What makes you say that?"

"Clearly you've already done some checking on me, so you know I haven't been there long enough to form attachments, or learn anything too incriminating. However, since on the surface it appears I'm on the outs with my wife, you figured I might be swayed into a little industrial espionage. Do I have that about right officers?"

"Not exactly doct... excuse me, Hal," Kimber submitted, "but close enough. We have compelling evidence that Omnium has been kidnapping people for their organs over the past decade at least. The problem, well one of many, is that no amount of evidence will result in a general indictment due to their contracts and high-level protection."

Hal thought a moment and then formed a quizzical look on his face. "So how does any request you're about to make *not* equate to my earlier deduction?"

"Because it's really more like sabotage rather than espionage doc," Jon said cynically.

"I see." Hal took another drink of his beer and waited for the inevitable proposal. His instincts told him they were on the same path he had begun the previous evening, but he suspected there were details they had yet to reveal.

"What level of risk are we talking about here? My job? Or even my life?"

Kimber sighed while trying to decide how much to reveal. She chose to lay it all out for him, leaving nothing to the imagination.

She explained the deaths of both Shepard and Navoa, as well as what happened at Omnium's Presidio office, where she shocked Jon confirming that she and Hal had indeed spotted each other near the Presidio Club. The pertinent points from her conversation with Gilad were touched on, and she summarized her harrowing chase from the Truckee Labs the day before, following the receipt of Shepard's tricorder from Leyton.

"Hidden inside that piece of memorabilia was a series of codes that we're convinced will gain access to files separating the willing participants and the not-so-willing," she concluded.

"Convinced? So you don't actually know what it's for? Seems like a lot to hedge your careers on for a code that may not do anything close to what you think it does."

"Perhaps, but my job is to find missing people, and I strongly suspect Omnium has been responsible for many of them since the unit was created seven years ago. The homeless, mentally ill, and the elderly have all fallen victim to a loophole in the Population Control Act. I probably don't have to tell you this, but veterans make up a substantial portion of those groups."

Hal finished his beer and sat back on the stack of boxes he used for a seat. It didn't take him long to respond to Kimber's last point.

"Paraphrasing what one of my mentors in med school told me; 'no one can prosper if anyone is exploited. Life must be valued above all else.' What is it you need me to do?"

"Well, in my experience, the simplest plans tend to have the better chance for success. Find a terminal this data stick with the copied sequence will work on, and send whatever contents are revealed to someone, or multiple someones, we can all agree on," Kimber instructed.

"We were thinking about sending it to a reputable journalist," Jon cut in, "but we wanted to clear it with you first before making any concrete arrangements."

"Reputable and journalist aren't terms I hear together often," Hal breathed as he rubbed his eyes. "Why not send it to one of Omnium's competitors, or even the Justice Department? Whomever the evidence goes to, assuming it *is* evidence, should at least be outside the reach of regional governors. The state's short-sighted progressiveness got us into this mess in the first place. Outside jurisdictions have a better chance of digging us out now. 'Us' as in those who have a better concept of ethics that is; hopefully anyway."

The officers looked at Hal wide-eyed for a moment, and then came to the conclusion that he was probably correct. Jon proposed to use all three options, to which the three agreed unless something better came along.

Over the next couple hours, and beers, they hashed out a plan that would provide each of them a role to play. Hal's piece would require the most risk, as he would be the one to actually connect with Omnium's system. Kimber was to follow up on the legal aspects of the case. Jon's role to secure specific sources to leak the information to was nearly as crucial, in order to efficiently disseminate the company's offenses.

~

After the officers departed, Hal finished the last of the beer in his flat as he turned the data stick with the coded sequence around his fingers. Not the only copy they assured him, but as he watched it dance in his hand he wondered how valuable it really was.

All of his efforts to get adequate sleep were for naught. How did I get myself into this? he asked himself repeatedly. In just a few hours, he would start the third day of his first job in four weeks, and if their mission was successful, there would be no fourth day, at least not at Omnium, he reminded himself with pseudo-confidence.

Worst case scenario, other than death, Hal presumed, would be that Omnium would be forced to close and, despite whistle-blower policies, he could potentially get black-listed to work at any other bio-tech company in the state. However he didn't have as much faith in some mysterious code as apparently the other two did.

While he knew full well that he'd be the most vulnerable of the trio, and his actions would likely delay reuniting with his family even longer, his conscience had already persuaded him that doing at least something to expose Omnium was the right thing to do.

He was reminded of a phrase his father told him when he faced choosing the easy way or the right way; "it's only the things you struggle for that have any real value."

Reminiscing about his childhood triggered Hal into thinking about Sean, and the times he said those same words to his own son. The flood of memories gave him a sense of euphoria that drifted him into a deep slumber.

A bit over four hours later, Hal's multiple alarms played their preset tones. Despite their music clashing with each other in an off-putting manner, he turned them off with a reverent look still prominent on his face.

Seventeen: Prospectus

She knew this wasn't part of the plan the three of them agreed upon the night before, but Kimber felt guilty about the completely imbalanced level of danger pressed upon Dr. Du... Hal.

As she approached the lift in the vacant underground lot once again, the doors parted much sooner than they should have, spilling its eerily bright light into the dusk-like parking area. The wall of mimic lights briefly froze as she did.

Three figures stood immersed in the white and appeared as featureless profiles in a triangular formation. Kimber remained motionless as the middle figure stepped into the space, revealing himself to be Chief Constable Fadil.

"What new business have you concocted to get in today inspector?" he asked in the bored, pompous way he talks to most people, Kimber assumed.

"I have a report regarding Dr. Leyton's former colleague to deliver. New information, old business," she bluffed.

Fadil blinked in a strangely robotic manner before responding. "Then you can provide me with this convenient news and I'll relay it appropriately."

"I would if that was the request given to me. Your boss lost a life-long friend; hardly an imminent security matter. Besides, aren't you also conducting your own inquest?"

"Your concern is touching, inspector, but he tends to not dwell in the past. We consider the case closed."

"Dwell? This happened four days ago! Are you really going to deny him some level of closure because I didn't make an appointment? Besides, I've seen his wall of collectables. It seems to me that he has a fondness for the past."

Fadil stared at her for a long, agonizing minute, then annoyingly looked away as he tugged on his uniform shirt in a vain attempt to straighten it more than it already was.

"Very well, but this is your last appearance on this matter. Leave the tazer with Kirlan this time though; I've seen what happens in desperation," he answered indignantly.

A female guardsman departed the lift, possibly brought along to perform a pat-down should the need arise, Kimber thought, and she handed her FCT-II to the other's outstretched hand. She boarded the lift with Fadil and another guardsman; the same stoic man from the previous two visits. The woman stayed behind in the cavernous, underground parking area.

Kimber was led down the now familiar hallway and through the handsome foyer. Leyton was staring intently at one of his many monitors and was taken aback when he noticed her presence.

"Inspector, did we hire you and nobody informed me?"

"He let me in," she countered as she jabbed her thumb over her shoulder to the vacated space where Fadil had stood. Why stick around when he probably has listening devices all over this room, she thought.

"I'll still inquire with HR in any case," Sidney said sarcastically. "What is the matter du jour?"

"I have some additional details concerning the death of Dr. Shepard, if you're interested."

Leyton turned to face her directly with a puzzled, almost offended look. "Why wouldn't I be interested? I've admitted to our growing divide, but we've still been friends and colleagues for over forty years."

Kimber held up her hands defensively, "just testing doctor." She walked over to his carved stone desk and placed her fingers on it, which gave her an idea. "The new data I brought is in video format. May I?" she asked gesturing to the desk.

~

Hal had begun to receive curious stares as he paced the lab, so he tried to make himself look busy by working on some virtual training. There were probably enough online lessons to keep him occupied for several months, so the simple matter of choosing one might be just as time consuming as doing one of the trainings themselves.

The course he selected happened to be a history of the company and its facilities. Hal scanned the session checklist to find a map of the grounds. He didn't notice a current one; the map offered was close to two years old, so he opened a new tab and pulled up a map via the employee intranet.

He carefully searched the interactive guide for anywhere that could help him. There were hundreds of company-registered computer terminals throughout the campus, but only a few that accepted data chip downloads/uploads for security reasons.

Not surprisingly, the executive and procurement offices had one or two full-system access machines, as well as security. There were, however, two other terminals located within *highly* conspicuous spaces: the service lounge by the landing port and outside the dining hall.

Hal sat back in his seat and sighed. Both of those locations were adjacent to the most public places on the campus, and were likely heavily surveilled as well. He pinched the bridge of his nose, to help allay the mounting tension, when suddenly a hand clapped down on his shoulder.

The shock nearly caused him to jolt out of his seat, but the firm grip prevented that. He slowly turned to appraise the hand, and then whom it was connected to, while also preparing a convincing explanation. Hal slumped in relief when he saw Drinian grinning at him, his hand still weighing him down.

"I think a *hello* is more customary," Hal quipped as he exited the map tab on his computer.

"I've never been one for customs. Not appropriate ones anyway. You ready to go doc?"

"Go? And leave this enthralling hive?"

"If you can tear yourself away, we have another assignment," Drinian answered, a grin still showing, though this one had a mischievous undertone. "This time though, we'll be making a delivery."

Hal blinked at him and pondered letting Drinian know about his encounter the previous night. The tech could be almost completely absolved, and the excursion may offer Hal a way out if connecting the data stick to the system alerts in one of a dozen ways. He got up and grabbed his jacket.

"I have to make a stop on the way to the port, but it shouldn't take long. Where are we going?"

"We've got a few containers of product to drop off at Groom Lake."

"Groom? Why do I recognize that name?"

Drinian's smile changed to a sly smirk. "Some people refer to it as Area 51, but us cultured folk call it Homey Airport or Groom Lake."

"So you're not one for customs but you're still cultured?" Hal joked as they exited the lab.

"Of course I am! You wouldn't believe the number of women who've told me to get lost in their native tongue. I'll go prep the ship and you go do whatever it is you need to do."

"Right. What will I be doing this time exactly?" Hal asked nervously, not making eye contact with anyone they passed in the hallways.

"Ah yes. You'll have the very important job of keeping me company. It may not look it but I can be very hard to entertain," Drinian answered, the playful grin back in full force.

Hal shook his head, thankful for the break in tedium at the office and distraction from the worry of his so-called sabotage. There couldn't have been a more opportune pretext to stop off at the port computer if he'd tried to come up with one. "Sounds good. See you in a few."

~

Miles Shepard's recorded confessional had ended and Sidney Leyton continued to stare at the vacant space in disbelief. Several seconds went by before Kimber felt the need to keep Leyton in that susceptible frame of mind.

"Judging by your reaction doctor, I'm going to presume that this is your first time viewing Dr. Shepard's last words. I'm also thinking you're mostly unaware of what he is accusing Omnium of doing. If true, that begs the question of who is really running this company, and why are they keeping facts from their own chief financial officer?"

Sidney was unmoved in his chair, still staring where the projection of Miles previously appeared. Kimber had to visually check that the man was still breathing before prodding him again, but thankfully she didn't have to.

"You know inspector, you've already asked me that question."

Kimber thought back to their first conversation. She had asked him about who's in charge, but he side-stepped even *that* answer with the skill of a politician.

"Yes doctor, and as I recall you didn't provide an answer that would satisfy a seasoned, apathetic journalist. However, your response isn't as important as what you're willing to do to either confirm or confute Dr. Shepard's claims."

Leyton slumped lower in his chair and released a subjugated sigh. He turned a weary look of resignation toward her in a mechanical manner.

"And what would you have me do inspector? Like I said before, I'm kept in the dark more than not, but I still have a job to do, and I'd prefer to continue doing it."

"All I'm asking, for the moment, is to venture a bit more through the rabbit hole and allow me to upload something on your computer. Dr. Shepard may have left you a last request."

~

Hal parted ways from Drinian and uneasily probed his pockets as he approached the port terminal. He located the data stick and took a deep breath. The computer's motion sensors detected his presence and Omnium's logo was projected all around him in the partially enclosed booth.

He quickly prepared the machine to read from a portable device and placed the stick on the reader tray.

Nothing happened. Hal saw the telltale lights that signified his stick being read through one open eye, but he began to feel silly squinting and holding his breath.

After a few tense seconds passed, a prompt appeared that indicated a folder was found and he was asked what he wanted to do with it; open or download to an external device. Hal selected the latter and a short moment later the download indicated completion. He retrieved the data stick and casually made his way to the double doors that led to the port.

The second set of doors hissed open as the first slid closed and Hal stopped in his tracks. An alarm began sounding and it seemed to come from all directions. Some of the lighting changed color as well, which directed those lagging about back to their designated work areas or certain public spaces.

He looked around both the lounge and the port for any threatening movement, but all he saw were security personnel rushing toward one of the landing pads. Three more guardsmen bumped past him, nearly knocking him over. Despite the lights, announcements, and brusque security staff telling him otherwise, he decided to see what the effort was all about.

~

A holographic prompt regarding an unnamed folder shimmered above Sidney's desk. Kimber wanted to glimpse the files prior to downloading, but before she gave the command to open it Leyton's office door opened with two guardsmen spilling through quite anxiously, speed-walking to Sidney's desk.

"We have a security breach Dr. Leyton," Fadil announced, his long stride putting him several paces in front of his deputy. "One of our technicians has absconded with some military-grade product and is attempting to launch from the port in his utility vehicle."

Almost as if a switch had turned in Sidney's head, he went from being completely focused on the mysterious file to the pragmatic business man in the blink of an eye.

"What product? What's being done to secure our intellectual property?" Leyton rose and cleared his desk. He stopped to appraise his security chief, and waited for an answer.

"We've activated the magnetic mooring fields in the entire bank of the landing platforms around the offending vessel, but his transport has been heavily modified and the fields are proving insufficient," Fadil answered after a delay due to his surprise at Sidney's quick reaction.

"To compensate I've instructed all available guardsmen to use restraining cables, and our Special Response Team is in route with heavier weaponry if that fails, sir."

"I see," Leyton replied, as he walked around his desk and explored his wall for the appropriate monitors. "That still doesn't answer my first question, and whose craft are we talking about here?"

"The pilot in question is Technician Drinian Posey, and you won't find him on the security feed doctor. He's uploaded a looped recording somehow. It's been reported that he has stolen our supply of advanced synaptic implants, sir."

Sidney stopped futilely trying to locate the port security feed and stared wide-eyed at his security chief. A combination of dread and fury filled his face.

"Would these be the same ASIs that were ordered liquidated more than two years ago, constable?"

"They would be. The Board overruled you sir. Too great a loss in regulated technology and potential revenue, in their opinion. If my report is satisfactory doctor, we must be getting to the port."

The pair synchronously spun on their heels and made their way to the exit. Leyton hesitated a second and then jogged to catch up. Kimber looked around the newly-emptied office, and then attempted to access Sidney's computer herself.

The terminal proved unresponsive to both verbal and manual commands. Once she realized his computer was locked out, she seized her copy of Shepard's code within the data stick and dashed after the others. They were already well-past the foyer and moving rapidly, so she scoffed and quickened her pace even more to catch them.

EIGHTEEN: ALL ABOARD

Hal continued to weave his way around the landing pads at Omnium's main port; keeping as much distance between himself and the gaggle of guardsmen he followed as he could without losing them in the chase.

The commotion he heard got incrementally louder and he knew he was growing close. He rounded one more pad with a stationary transport and there it was; Drinian's ship besieged by nearly twenty guardsmen trying to tether it with cable.

Hal wrestled his way around the craft to try and get a glimpse into the cockpit. When he made it to the bow, Hal was shocked to find a calm and smiling Drinian peering back at him. His mobile began to ring and Hal went agape at the display on his watch before he answered.

"What the hell are you doing Drinian? What is going on?"

"What took you so long doc? We're on a bit of a schedule here, so if you don't mind disrupting the tie job they're trying to do out there before you board, it would really help our odds for a smoother getaway."

"Getaway? Are you mad?! How do you expect to get away from all this, even *with* my help?"

"Eh, I'm not too worried about them. I'm more concerned about you getting hurt in the fray. And trust me when I say I'm doing the right thing; I owe you one and I'd hate for you to miss out on that. So are you coming or not?"

~

Kimber finally reached the trio ahead of her but barely kept pace with them. She was only able to eavesdrop on parts of the tongue-lashing Leyton dispensed to Fadil, but it was clear to her he was upset and concerned those implants weren't destroyed long ago, as he requested.

She was also impressed by the level of self-control Fadil was showing by not responding to Sidney's rant in the least; by the looks of him from behind that is.

They arrived at the pandemonium that had become the port, and despite the raised voices and varied threats to the pilot, the scene seemed fairly organized to her.

The first words Kimber heard out of Fadil's mouth since they departed Leyton's office was for her and Sid to stay out of the way, but her attention was too focused on Hal in front of the beleaguered craft to heed the order.

Despite pleas to remain where she was, Kimber circumnavigated the efforts to secure the transport as best she could. She approached within ear-shot of Hal and noticed that he was on his mobile. He turned, and after a few seconds to register what he saw, gave her a look of surprise and suspicion.

Kimber opened her mouth to assure him of her presence when a hand clamped down on her shoulder like a vise. On instinct, she grabbed the hand and spun her body toward the hand's owner on her left foot, and kicked at the person's kneecap hard with her right.

The distinctive wet-pop could still be heard over the noise at the port, which indicated something had broken. The woman yelped in agony and fell to the ground. Kimber recognized the writhing guardsman as the one she surrendered her weapon to at the garage.

The painful cries did not go unnoticed by the surrounding security staff. Three of them stopped trying to secure the ship and rushed to the aid of their fallen comrade.

Kimber knelt beside the woman and began patting around for her FCT-II. She located it in a side-pocket on the guardsman's good leg. Once the woman realized what Kimber was doing she yelled out to her advancing associates.

Their pace quickened and Kimber backed up into a defensive stance. "Stand fast! She startled me and I reacted improperly. It was an accident," she pleaded.

The three slowed synchronously. One bent over to check on their injured mate and the other two kept watch. They all eyed her suspiciously but said nothing. Almost mechanically, the two standing watch put their hands to their ears; a habit of the inexperienced with earpieces as they received communications.

Kimber's adrenalin had briefly subsided after talking down the near stand-off, but it was working its way back into her system. The squad had been given new orders and advanced on her again, reaching for their sidearms.

She unfolded her tazer and fired at the two ready to draw down on her. They jerked-slumped limply to the ground with a thud. The third thought twice about drawing his weapon, but the scuffle got the interest of even more guardsmen and Kimber knew she was about to be outgunned, with only seven stun bolts left.

~

Hal saw the situation take a dangerous turn, but he was still too slow to react. By the time he made his way to Kimber's side, she had stunned two people and held another at bay, with more on their way.

"They're about to regroup and detain the both of you," Drinian announced in Hal's ear. "I don't know who she is, but you might want to bring her along if you're coming with me."

Hal knew his options were quickly vanishing. Too many people saw him to avoid a personal search followed by a few uncomfortable conversations. He didn't want to leave Kimber to suffer the same fate, so he further improvised their plan.

"Turn your van thirty degrees port, and open your starboard hatch," Hal instructed Drinian. "Prepare for your best speed!"

Hal checked to see if Drinian got the message and saw that the ship began to slowly rotate, easily moving despite the retention cables.

"Time for plan C it seems inspector. Our escape route is clear, let's move!"

"Plan C? What was plan B? How does that utility van expect to break those cables *and* constrictors?" Kimber asked with her attention still on the approaching guardsmen.

"Plan B must've been what brought you here unexpectedly. And don't worry, you can trust the pilot; at least that's what he tells me. He owes me it seems."

Hal had to practically drag Kimber to get her to move, but she still kept a watchful eye on their accumulating foes.

The tension in the restraining cables could be heard as an almost musical hum; as if they were giant cello strings. They reached the edge of Drinian's van and a hail-fire of tazer bolts began peppering the hull and air around them.

Kimber popped off two shots and they both crouch-ran to the open hatch. Hal dove into the quaint cabin and spun around to reach for Inspector Lee. She was two paces away when her eyes went wide and she fell into his grasp.

Hal pulled her close, hooked his left arm around her back, and heaved her inside as he yelled to Drinian to lift off.

The engines crescendoed and the cables snapped with a twang. Mooring fields slowed their ascent briefly, but once they were out of range, the craft lurched forward like they were being pulled by a rope that just became taught.

Hal breathed a sigh of relief. He wiped his brow and realized his hand was wet with blood. "Inspector? Lee, talk to me. You doing ok?"

"Ugh. Other than this stinging in my back I think I'll make it. Where are we going?"

"Uh, good question. Let me look at that pain in the back. You seem to be leaking. Hey, Drinian? What is our destination?"

"I wasn't joking when I said we have product for Groom Lake," Drinian answered as he turned around to face his passengers. "The part I left out is those particular products were meant to be sold to the highest bidder... no matter who that may be. I made other plans for them."

Kimber lay on her stomach so Hal could check her wound. There was something stuck in her jacket. It was a projectile he was unfamiliar with. He plucked it and rolled it around in his fingers, examining the cylindrical device.

"Is your jacket a type of body armor?" Hal asked as he analyzed the object.

Kimber winced with each bump of turbulence. "Yeah, high-impact reactive flex-fiber. Did it not stop whatever struck me?"

"It did, most of it anyway. Can you take it off so I can patch you up?"

There was a short struggle with the garment, but Hal gasped when he saw the injury.

"The good news is your blood loss appears to be minor. What troubles me is this wound. It seems to have turned the tissue around it a grey color, and it's more inflamed than I anticipated. Have you seen a bullet like this before?"

She sat upright and took the item from over her shoulder. "I don't recognize it. You pulled this thing out of my jacket?"

Hal side-stepped the question and asked Drinian about it. Kimber tossed it to him with another painful flinch.

"Damn," the pilot breathed. "Where did this come from?"

"My back apparently," Kimber responded as she craned her neck toward Hal. "Do you know what it is?"

"It's a tracking device, but instead of using a transmitter that can be detected and blocked it has a radioactive gel from a very unique isotope. Even low-orbit satellites can trace it, with proper instrumentation of course."

Hal and Kimber exchanged looks of concern and confusion. "So there's some radioactive goo in my body?"

"That's how it's designed," Drinian continued. "The projectile injects the stuff into its target, which is usually a vehicle of some sort, so it's more difficult to remove."

The passengers shared another glance, and Hal was entering unfamiliar territory. "Perhaps you should increase speed, and contact their tower. Stress that there may be a medical emergency," he said as he gave Kimber's darkening wound another tentative peek.

~

"No, I don't have a landing permit," explained an exasperated Drinian. "I just spoke with Lieutenant Grady a few minutes ago. Could you check with her about my clearance please?"

Hal couldn't hear what Homey Tower was relaying, but if he had to guess it was the all-too familiar dance of inflexible fortitude that all enlisted perform until told otherwise.

"You can take all the precautions you like, but when I said this was a medical emergency, perhaps I forgot to mention the patient is a California State Inspector. We're not going to deviate from this course, so your choice is to prepare for our arrival in any way you deem fit or shoot us down."

The van took a sharp downturn, which forced Hal to grab onto a storage locker's handle while also bracing Kimber. He wasn't sure what to be more concerned about; Drinian's ultimatum to a top secret military base or Kimber's survival.

A few tense moments passed, and the next thing Hal realized was that the engines were powering down. They all breathed a sigh of relief, though Kimber's was somewhat labored. He was about to re-check her vitals when the port hatch burst open and multiple M41 rifles were stuffed in his face.

The trio was separated with Hal and Drinian taken into custody and Kimber hauled away on a stretcher. Hal shouted to the med techs that he was a doctor and what Kimber's prognosis was, but their response was only a curt nod.

Four hours and two imperious interrogations later, a tight-lipped major was leading Hal to the infirmary. He guessed by all the grim faces that Kimber's condition wasn't especially promising; though it may also be due to low morale, Hal mused.

He entered the ominously outmoded operating room, and aside from some slight paleness, she looked perfectly healthy. Huh, perhaps the bleak looks really were a morale problem, Hal considered hopefully. Area 51 probably wasn't all that exciting to the people who worked there, he figured.

"I couldn't ask you to risk your job, and possibly life, without taking the same risks myself," Kimber said as quiet as a whisper when Hal reached her bedside. "I didn't even get a chance to upload the code."

"Plan B I presume?" Hal joked while he took a perfunctory glance at her monitors. All indicators appeared to be in the normal range. "Don't worry. I was able to download… something, onto my data stick. So the mission could be considered a success, if the thing wasn't confiscated by the Air Force that is."

Kimber seemed to be relieved by that disclosure. She then became reluctant to say what had to have been obvious by Hal's affectation. "They're not sure if I'm going to recover."

The news hit Hal like he had just jumped into freezing water. He couldn't move or speak, except his eyes, which darted to all the displays once more.

"They're confident all the radioactive material is out of my system, but it was so potent it did a great deal of damage. I need to swap out a few of my parts. Three guesses who the nearest company to do that is."

The irony was not lost on him. He knew there was no way Omnium would help them in time. Most major military bases had their own supply of regenerative tissue, but Hal was unsure if they would issue any to a civilian, assuming Area 51 even had any since it was primarily a research and development facility.

"Did any of the medical staff mention using some of their... parts?" he asked the very lethargic inspector.

"They don't carry any usable material, or so I'm told. I think they said something about applying stem tissue but I'm apparently past the point for a patch job."

Hal's mind reeled. He had dealt with injuries of vast varieties, as well as infections and even a few high-level contagions, but he didn't recall a time when he felt so helpless to do anything medically since his boot camp days. He took Kimber's clammy hand and fought the urge to cry.

"Inspector, I'll do what I can to make sure you get the transplants you need. And I will see to it that justice is done, for you and a decade of victims Omnium has wrought. I give you my word."

Kimber looked at him with bloodshot eyes. "No matter what happens to me, I know you'll do the right thing. You're a good man Dr. Dune. Be sure to get ahold of Jon for me. I don't think he knows what's going on yet. He doesn't know I went to Omnium."

Hal nodded and held her hand even tighter. She didn't seem to notice the increased grip, which only made his sorrow and despair even deeper.

Epilogue: Life Debts
Airborne near Yosemite National Park

An Omnium special response team transport sped across the Sierras from the failed pursuit of the treacherous techie's utility van. The craft held four SRT guardsmen in EDS suits led by Constable Fadil himself. Not only was it strange that the chief of security personally accompanied them on a mission instead of coordinating from the Labs, but the man had also spent the entire trip inside the private comms compartment.

"We don't know precisely how the personnel at Homey Airfield responded as of yet, but I can confirm the craft was not shot down," Fadil informed the trio of regional governors.

"The Defense Intelligence Agency must have a hand in this," RG Dolar of the Realign Region speculated. "They've been pleading for more oversight on our military products for years."

"If that's the case governors," Fadil continued, "then no amount of retribution on your part will likely assist in retrieving the ASIs. We may have to abandon that program."

"I'm afraid it's worse than that Fadil," RG Kirlan of the Lockheed Region interjected in a dire tone. "We've already received comm traffic from the DOJ about teams moving in on Omnium as we speak. We cannot allow you or *any* of your programs to come under their scrutiny. We're going to have to cancel them all to be sure."

Fadil inhaled deeply and held it over the realization of what that meant. "I understand sir. It's been my honor to serve you for the advancement of the California Republic."

The three RGs nodded and signed off. Fadil began to slowly exhale when an explosive device that all Omnium vehicles contained detonated, causing the transport to lose altitude. His lungs were emptied by the time the craft slammed into a heavily forested mountainside.

~

"There's a swift courier en route for Inspector Lee, Dr. Dune," Colonel Kithe began from behind his office desk, "but due to the moratorium on Omnium by Justice and

Homeland Security, it's coming from Vancouver instead I'm afraid. The detective from the SFPD you asked for might make it here before them."

Hal looked around the room like a kid in a candy store. The wall-to-wall shelves of models, which he presumed were of top-secret craft designed and tested here, was a sight to behold. Then he noticed how quiet the office was and turned to find the colonel waiting for a response.

"Uh, that's good to hear, thank you sir. Just one question though; how did the freeze on Omnium happen so quickly?"

Kithe sat back in his chair and plucked a small device off his desk. "Multiple reasons actually. Your pilot didn't choose this facility by happenstance. Despite our long history of experimental aircraft and related technology, after the war, parts of the base were converted to biotech research for military applications.

"Over the past seven or eight years, Omnium's operations became increasingly suspicious, and the rumors behind the Farlander incident convinced the DIA that they needed someone on the inside to validate a substantial investment the DOD made with them, covertly."

"Drinian," Hal said completing the colonel's line of thought.

"Yes, amongst others," Kithe said with an impressed grin. "Due to Mr. Posey's penchant for not keeping a low profile, as you no doubt noticed by his utility van, additional assets were greenlit."

"You seem to know a great deal about this operation Colonel. That could've been useful when we were trying to land."

"Yes, well, I'm one of a handful of COs who are in a position to know. To answer your question doctor, between reports from those agents, the implants that were just delivered by the three of you, and the contents of this data stick that you may recognize," Kithe held up the item he'd been shuffling around his fingers, "it's more than enough for the feds to finally get their hands dirty."

Hal nodded at the comment. "You guys do all the work, they get the glory. I've been there before. So what was on the chip?"

"That, I'm sorry to say, is the limit of exposition for the moment doctor. How we proceed may change that though."

Hal paused trying to sneak peeks at the models that surrounded him and gave the colonel a harried scowl. "Pardon me sir, but what are you talking about? I acquired the info on that stick, at great risk to myself I might add, and lost the only job I've had in a month for the effort. So I'm past caring about protocol if you don't mind."

"Your experience in thankless investigative work and familiarity with protocol is precisely why we're having this conversation, doctor, as well as Mr. Posey's recommendation for you to the DIA."

Hal scoffed. "My experience was as a non-contract agent for active-duty military; that hardly translates to industrial espionage with technology I'd only read about a few days ago. Where would I fit into that?"

"On top of the other highlights in your background, the fact that you're a medical doctor certainly helps, and that you can clearly adapt quickly. Otherwise you probably wouldn't be here."

Hal looked at his hands. He was surprised at how calm he was with this conversation. He had so many questions, but was strangely confident in the answers he already surmised, except three.

"Where would I live, where would I work, and how would my agreeing to this affect my family?"

"I don't have a specific answer to your second point, just that it involves the Forensic

Psych Division of the Bureau of Prisons and National Institute of Mental Health. But regarding the other two you can keep your apartment in San Francisco if you like, and as for your family… excuse me a moment."

The colonel took a call on his desk phone that Hal couldn't hear the content of, except Kithe's side of the conversation as well as his mannerisms.

"I see. And you're confident you did everything you could? Very well, please make the appropriate arrangements."

The man sighed and ran his hand through his high-and-tight haircut. He took his time meeting Hal's eyes. The reluctance and sorrow was palpable.

"I'm sorry doctor. Inspector Lee didn't make it."

Hal had the urge to jump out of his chair and curse everything and everyone, but his despair kept him seated. His mind raced at what he could have done differently. He barely knew the woman but she gave him the same sense that the Marines he served with did; a bond he felt he owed a debt to. Because of this, there was only one response he could summon…

"Colonel, count me in."

"Good to hear Dr. Dune. In that case, let me fill you in about advanced synaptic implants, and the nearly fifty-thousand people Omnium essentially *stole* body parts from over the past decade alone."

To Be Continued...